Meet
at the Chapel

———

Joanna Sims

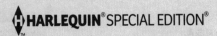

Recycling programs
for this product may
not exist in your area.

ISBN-13: 978-0-373-65983-8

Meet Me at the Chapel

Copyright © 2016 by Joanna Sims

Printed in U.S.A.

"It'd be a shame. You coming out all this way just to go home so soon."

"I know," Casey replied. "But I can't impose on my sister for the summer—not now."

"That's right," he agreed. Then added, "I have a loft apartment above the barn. It's a little rough, but it's livable."

Casey looked at Brock and listened while he continued.

"The way you are with Hannah—it's pretty impressive. And it got me thinking that we could help each other out. Hannah does fine with academics—she's even strong in math and science. But it's her..."

"Pragmatics," she filled in for him.

He glanced at her again. "Exactly. How 'bout I let you use the loft for the summer in exchange for some private social-language support. How does that set with you?"

Casey stared at Brock's profile. "Are you serious?"

"Yeah. Why? Do you think it's a bad idea?"

"Heck no, I don't think it's a bad idea. I think it's a pretty genius idea."

* * *

THE BRANDS OF MONTANA:
Wrangling their own happily-ever-afters

Dear Reader,

Thank you for choosing *Meet Me at the Chapel*. This is my seventh Special Edition book featuring the Brand family. Amazing! Brock McAllister and Casey Brand's journey to finding lasting love was a joy to write. Casey is an independent special education teacher whose favorite companion is a micro-teacup poodle, Hercules, and Brock is a soon-to-be single-father ranch foreman fighting for custody of his daughter with autism. This is a friends-fall-in-love story filled with beautiful imagery, tender moments and, of course, romance!

In *Meet Me at the Chapel*, you will encounter old friends from previous Brand books. It just wouldn't be a Brands of Montana book if Hank and Barbara Brand didn't make an appearance. They have been in all seven Brand stories! I love writing about the Brand family because I have an opportunity to unearth my fond childhood memories of Montana and give them a new life in the pages of my books. What a blessing!

I invite you to visit my website, joannasimsromance.com, and while you're there, be sure to sign up for *Rendezvous Magazine* for Brand family extras, news and swag. Part of the joy of writing is hearing from readers. If you write me, I will write you back! That's a promise.

Happy Reading!

Joanna

Joanna Sims is proud to pen contemporary romance for Harlequin Special Edition. Joanna's series, The Brands of Montana, features hardworking characters with hometown values. You are cordially invited to join the Brands of Montana as they wrangle their own happily-ever-afters. And, as always, Joanna welcomes you to visit her at her website: joannasimsromance.com.

Books by Joanna Sims

Harlequin Special Edition

The Brands of Montana

High Country Baby
High Country Christmas
A Match Made in Montana
Marry Me, Mackenzie!
The One He's Been Looking For
A Baby for Christmas

Visit the Author Profile page
at Harlequin.com for more titles.

Dedicated to Aa and MM

Thank you for allowing me to use your proposal as inspiration. Congratulations on your engagement!

Chapter One

"Recalculating."

Casey Brand had been lost in thought until the portable GPS interrupted her daydream. She tightened her grip on the steering wheel of the moving truck, hands placed firmly at ten and two, before she glanced at the GPS screen.

"Recalculating."

"No!" Casey argued with the machine. "We are *not* recalculating!"

"Recalculating."

The map on the screen of the GPS had disappeared, replaced by a single word: *searching*. She hadn't been to her uncle and aunt's ranch since she was a teenager, so finding it by memory wasn't a viable option. She needed the GPS to do its job. Casey took her eyes off the road for a second to tap the screen of the GPS.

"*Darn* it!" She was going to have to pull over.

Her trip from Chicago to Montana had been fraught with setbacks: violent thunderstorms, road construction, bad food, horrible menstrual cramps and a rental truck that struggled to maintain speed on every single hill. Not wanting to risk stopping on an incline, Casey punched the gas pedal several times to help the truck make the climb to the top of the hill.

"Come on, you stupid truck!" Casey rocked back and forth in her seat. "You can do it!"

Halfway to the top of the hill, the check-engine light flashed and then disappeared.

"Don't you *dare*!" Casey ordered.

Three quarters of the way up the hill, the orange check-engine light appeared and, this time, it stayed.

Casey groaned in frustration. With every tedious mile, it felt like the universe was telling her that her trip was ill-fated. At the top of the hill, she turned on her blinker, carefully eased the truck onto the gravelly berm and shifted into Park.

"Recalculating."

"Oh, just shut up," Casey grumbled as she shut off the engine.

"You wait here," she said to the teacup poodle watching her curiously from inside a dog carrier that was secured with a seat belt. "I'll be right back."

She pulled on the lever to pop the hood and jumped out of the cab. At the front of the truck, she was immediately hit with a strong, acrid smell coming from the engine. The hood of the truck was hot to the touch; Casey yanked her baseball cap off her head and used it to protect her fingers while she lifted up the hood.

"Holy cannoli!" Casey covered her face with the

cap and backed away from the truck. A moment later, she ran back to the cab of the truck and grabbed the dog carrier, before she put distance between herself and the rental.

A small electrical fire had melted several wires in the engine; it looked as if the fire had already put itself out, but she couldn't risk driving the truck now. For the time being, she was stuck on a desolate road, with her sister's worldly possessions in the back of the broken-down rental, a teacup poodle and angry black storm clouds forming overhead.

Casey pulled her phone out of the back pocket of her jeans to call her sister.

"Come on, Taylor…pick up the phone."

When Taylor didn't answer, she called again. She was on her third attempt when a fat raindrop landed on the bridge of her nose. She looked up at the black cloud that was now directly above her.

"Really?" she asked the cloud.

Her sister wasn't answering, for whatever reason, so she needed to move on to plan B. She was about to dial her aunt Barbara's cell number when she noticed a horse and rider galloping across a field on the opposite side of the road. She didn't think, she reacted.

"Hey!" Casey ran across the road, waving her free arm wildly. "Hey!"

The rider didn't seem to hear her or see her. At the edge of the road, Casey looked down at her beloved Jimmy Choo crushed leather Burke boots and then at the rider. There was mud and grass and rock between her and the rustic wooden fence that surrounded the wide, flat field. Her boots had only known city sidewalks and shopping malls. She didn't want her beautiful boots to get dirty, but there wasn't a choice—she had to get the rider's attention. She ran, as softly as she could manage, through the mud and wet grass to the fence. She put the dog carrier on the ground so she could climb up onto the fence.

"Hey!" Casey yelled again and waved her hat in the air. *"Help!"*

This time, the rider, a cowboy by the look of him, saw her. He slowed his muscular black horse, assessed the situation and then changed direction.

"He sees us!" Casey told her canine companion. The closer the cowboy came, the more familiar he seemed. Casey stared harder at the man galloping toward her, sitting so confident and erect in the saddle.

"Wait a minute. I *know* you!"

Brock McAllister was galloping toward home, racing the rain clouds gathering to the west, when he spotted a woman perched on his fence, waving her arm to get his attention. Brock slowed his stallion and assessed the situation before he decided to change direction. As he came closer, he could see that the woman wasn't as young as he had thought. She had a slight build, borderline thin, and appeared to be in her midthirties.

"Brock! It's me—Casey," the woman called out to him with another wave. "Casey Brand."

The moment Casey added the last name "Brand" to the equation, Brock made the connection. He had worked on the Brand family's ranch, Bent Tree, since he was a teenager, and had worked his way up to ranch foreman. Taylor, Casey's older sister, was married to his stepbrother, Clint, and had just given him a niece. So he'd heard through the grapevine that Casey was coming to Montana to help her sister with the new baby, but he hadn't given her much thought one way or the other until he found her climbing on his fence.

Lightning lit up the gray clouds hanging over the mountains in the distance and the once-sporadic raindrops were coming with more frequency. He only had a few short minutes to stay ahead of the storm. If Casey needed rescuing, it was going to have to be quick.

"You have perfect timing!" Casey gave him a relieved smile when he halted his horse next to the fence. "Would you believe it? The engine caught on fire!"

Given that information, Brock made a split-second decision that he couldn't leave Casey behind in the rental while he went back to the farm to get his truck.

"We need to get out of the way of this storm." Brock walked his horse in a small circle so he could get closer to the fence.

"Is there someone you can call to come get me? I tried my sister, but she didn't answer."

"You can't stay here. We're under a tornado watch." Brock halted his horse and held out his gloved hand to Casey. "You need to come with me. *Now!*"

It seemed to him that his words hadn't registered. She stared at him with a stunned expression, but didn't budge.

"Come on!" Brock yelled at her, his large stallion prancing anxiously in place. "Give me your hand!"

The urgency in his voice, along with a clap of thunder, finally got her moving. But instead of giving him her hand, she gave him her dog carrier.

"Hold Hercules! I've got to get my wallet!"

Surprised, Brock reached out his hand to take the carrier before his brain had a chance to register that there was a miniature dog, the smallest dog he'd ever seen, inside of the designer bag.

"What the hell…?" Brock's low baritone voice was caught on a gust of wind. While he waited for Casey's return, Brock raised the carrier to eye level so he could get a better look at his new passenger. "What in the heck are you supposed to be?"

Casey ran on the treadmill regularly, so running the short distance to the truck and back was easy for her. She grabbed her wallet then locked the door. Brock's stallion was chomping at the bit, refusing to stand still by the fence.

"Easy, Taj…" She heard Brock trying to calm the horse while he circled back to the fence. On her way to the truck, the first raindrops had landed on the top of her head and on the tip of her nose. By the time she'd climbed back to the top of the fence, it had begun to rain in earnest. Casey straddled the fence while Brock steadied the prancing, overly excited stallion that was tossing his head and biting at the bit.

"Come on!" Brock ordered. "Use the stirrup!"

Casey grabbed ahold of the damp material of the cowboy's chambray shirt, slipped her left foot into the stirrup and swung her right leg over the horse's rump. Casey tucked Hercules under one arm and held on tight to Brock with the other. The heavy sheets of rain were being pushed at an angle by the wind, strong enough and hard enough that the right side of her face felt as if it were being pelted by rock salt. She tried to shield Hercules as much as she could from the rain while she tried to protect her own face by tucking her head into Brock's back.

Casey pressed her head into the cowboy's back, and tightened her arms around his waist. In her youth, she had been an excellent rider; she knew how to sit and she knew how to balance her weight on the back of a horse. So, even though his stallion had an extra burden to carry, the impact on the horse would be minimal. Loud claps of thunder followed the lightning strikes by only a few seconds, signaling to Casey that the lightning was too close for comfort. Riding on horseback in a lightning storm was an invitation to be struck.

"Yah, Taj!" she heard Brock yell as he leaned forward and prodded the sure-footed stallion. The stallion leapt forward and kicked his speed into an even higher gear.

Casey squeezed her eyes shut and concentrated on following the movement of Brock's body. All of her senses were being bombarded at once: the masculine scent of leather and sweat on Brock's shirt mingled with the earthy, sweet scent of the rain, the feel of Brock's thick thigh muscles pressed so tightly against her own, and the sound of the stallion's hooves pounding the ground as it carried them across the flat, grassy plain. When she heard what sounded like hooves hitting gravel, she opened her eyes. From beneath the brim of her baseball cap, she saw part of a denim-blue house with a flat roof and a white trim through a canopy of trees.

On their way up the narrow gravel driveway, they passed a faded brown barn and older-model blue-and-yellow Ford tractor. Now in full view, Brock's two-story house was square with two bay windows and kitty-corner steps leading up to covered porches on either side. Brock halted the stallion directly in front of the stairs, a maneuver Casey suspected he'd done many times before.

"Get inside. The door's unlocked!" Brock ordered. "I'll be back in a minute."

Brock held the carrier while she dismounted; once she was safely on the ground, he handed Hercules to her. She ran up the steps, and kept on running until she reached the shelter of the covered porch by the front door. She wiped the water off her face as best she could, but her clothing and hair and boots were sopping wet and her skin was wet beneath the material of her jeans and shirt. She hesitated by the door, not wanting to drip water all over his floor. But she heard Brock yelling at her as he dismounted, telling her to get inside. Casey took one last look at the blackened sky filled with swirling gray clouds pouring rain before she followed his direction and opened the front door to the farmhouse.

The heavy door swung open and Casey crossed the threshold into Brock's dark world. The house was old—she estimated by the look of the lead-stained glass windows abutting the front door that it had already celebrated its centennial birthday. But it had not celebrated in grand fashion. The curtains were made of a dark cherry brocade and were drawn shut to block out any light. Cornflower blue wallpaper dotted with small white flowers contrasted oddly with the forest green shag carpet. Casey knew from her sister that Brock was separated from his wife, Shannon. Brock and Shannon had been "an item" all through middle school and high school. Shannon had been a Miss Montana first runner-up and Casey could remember looking at her when she was a preteen and thinking that Shannon was the prettiest person she'd ever seen. They had married right after high school and the marriage had produced a daughter. But, according to Taylor, they were going through a messy divorce and custody battle and Shannon had been living in California with her new boyfriend.

Yes, Shannon was probably still a very beautiful woman—but she wasn't a housekeeper. Everything in the house seemed dingy and tired—in need of a good scrubbing to get rid of the wet-dog smell and a serious cleaning in general. Yet Casey could look past the clutter and floral decor to see the potential in the house. The dark, carved woodwork used for the crown molding, the built-in bookshelves and the stairwell, which appeared to be original to the house and beautifully made. The bay windows with those antique stained-glass windows were stunning. Even though the house seemed to be sagging beneath the weight of disrepair, with a lot of TLC, it could be something truly special.

"It's going to be okay." Casey put the carrier down on the ground so she could kneel down and take off her boots. No sense just standing there making a puddle in Brock's foyer. Casey took inventory of her options and then took Hercules, carrier and all, through the living room until she had reached what appeared to be the middle of the house.

"You wait here," she told Hercules; her pocket poodle had shocked her by not making a sound, even during his first jarring ride on a horse.

Casey went to a small bathroom just off the living room.

"Jackpot." Casey found a stack of clean, mismatched towels jammed under the sink.

She quickly dried her thick, waist-length hair before twisting it into the towel like a turban. With a second towel, she got the excess water off her shirt and jeans before ripping off her socks so she could stand on the damp towel in her bare feet.

Outside, the wind was howling around the house, sending loose leaves swirling past the window. The trees were starting to bend from the force of the wind and rain, which hadn't let up since they arrived at the ranch.

What was keeping Brock?

As if on cue, Brock burst through the front door and slammed it shut behind him. Not bothering to take off his wet boots, he strode into the living room and turned on the television. The severe-weather bulletin that had trumped regular programing was running images of a funnel cloud that seemed to be too close for comfort.

"Stay here," he said as he turned off the television.

Brock took the narrow stairs up to the second floor two at a time. He went to the master bedroom, tugged one of the plaid shirts down off the bedpost, then grabbed a pair of his soon-to-be ex-wife's jeans and socks out of a dresser drawer. He needed to get his unexpected guest taken care of before he went to go get his daughter, Hannah, who was at a friend's house roughly fifteen minutes away. He had to get to Hannah.

"They're clean." He pushed the clothes into her arms.

Casey was still trying to process the fact that she was caught up in a tornado situation, when Brock swung open a door that led to a cellar. A blast of stale air hit her in the face.

Brock switched on a battery-powered light. "Change and then you and your dog need to go down to the cellar. There's a weather radio down there, along with other supplies. Switch it on so you know what's happening. Wait there until I get back."

"You're leaving?" There was the tiniest crack in her voice. She was accustomed to blizzards, but tornadoes were an entirely different kind of natural menace.

"I'm going to get my daughter!" he hastened to say. And then he was gone.

She followed his directions—they were sensible and were meant to keep her safe. She stripped out of her wet clothes, wrung them out and hung them over the tub. The plaid shirt was huge on her—she rolled the sleeves up several times so her hands were free. Likewise, the jeans were loose around the waist and hips, and way too long. Casey folded the waistband down to make the jeans fit more securely, and then cuffed the bottom of the jeans so she could walk without stepping on them.

Once she was in dry clothes, she pulled the towel off her head and twisted her tangled hair into a topknot.

"Here goes nothing." Casey opted to breathe through her mouth to avoid inhaling the musty odor of the cellar. After some time down there, she hoped she wouldn't even notice it.

At the bottom of the rickety steps, Casey found a spot on the ground where she could unfold a blanket and hunker down until the coast was clear. The wind was so strong that it felt as if the house was swaying and groaning overhead.

"Come on out, little one." Casey opened the carrier and coaxed the rust-colored micro-poodle out onto the blanket.

She was glad that Hercules was content to curl up

in her lap, because she needed his company. He made her feel calmer. With a frustrated, self-pitying sigh, Casey turned on the weather radio and knew that the only thing she could do now was wait and pray.

"I'm so sorry, Brock." Kay Lynn opened the door to the trailer. "I had to call. I haven't seen her like this in a while. She was hitting herself and biting her hand again. She's been in a nosedive for the last hour or so."

"Is she in her normal spot?"

Kay Lynn nodded toward the hallway of the single-wide trailer. Brock walked quickly, but calmly, down the narrow hallway to the spare bedroom. Squeezed between a full-size bed and the wall, his twelve-year-old daughter was curled into a tight ball, rocking back and forth. In front of her, lying on top of Hannah's feet, was a golden Lab.

"Good girl, Ladybug." Brock knelt down, put his hand on the dog's head for a moment, before he reached out for his daughter's hand.

"Hannah," he said softly. "It's time to go home."

Hannah had been officially diagnosed with Asperger syndrome when she was eight. Her IQ was very high, but there were quirks to her personality that set her apart from other children her age. And, when a storm was coming, Brock always anticipated that she was going to have an off day. If he'd had any idea that she was going to spiral like this, he would have stayed home with her.

"Come on, baby girl." He directed the protective dog to move out of the way so he could help Hannah make the transition from the trailer to his truck. "We're going home."

Hannah lifted her head up. Her face, so much like his, was still damp from shed tears. His heart tightened every time his daughter cried. Brock wiped her tears from her cheeks before he lifted her up into his arms and hugged her tightly. The squeezing always calmed her.

"Why didn't you come sooner?" Hannah asked when he put her down.

"I got here as fast as I could." Brock took her hand in his. "Now, I need you to use your 'stay calm' plan on the way home. Okay?"

Hannah nodded. "Come on, Lady."

Now that he had his daughter with him, Brock felt complete. He could handle anything, as long as he had his daughter by his side. He could even handle a messy divorce from Shannon, Hannah's mother. They were in a custody battle for Hannah and had been for nearly a year. Shannon wanted to move Hannah out to California with her, and it was going to happen over his dead carcass. Hannah was going to stay in Montana, with him, in the only home she'd ever known. Period.

"You'd better hunker down, Kay Lynn. You're a sitting duck out here. You could come with us, but you've got to come now."

Kay Lynn's silver-streaked hair blew around the sunken cheeks of her face. She waved her hand as if she could bat away the tornado with her rough-skinned fingers. "That tornado don't want none of me, Brock. You go on and get Hannah home. I'll be right as rain."

There was no sense wasting time trying to convince Kay Lynn to leave her home—she was as much a part of the prairie surrounding the old trailer as was the willowy Junegrass. He'd offered, but knew she wouldn't take him up on it.

With a quick wave to Hannah's sometimes babysitter, Brock bundled Hannah into the truck and headed back to his little Montana spread. They didn't see much more than a few drops of rain on their short drive back. Brock pulled into the gravelly driveway that led to their farmhouse knowing that they were in a lull. The clouds above were still churning and angry, and it was only a matter of time before the wind would start howling again. They were in the most dangerous time of a tornado, the time when many folks get fooled into thinking that the threat was over, when in actuality it was just about to begin.

Chapter Two

"It's time for our storm plan, Hannah. Tell me what we need to do." Brock pulled the screen door open to their house. The rain was still misty, but he knew from experience that that could change on a dime.

Hannah was faithfully rattling off the steps of their storm plan when they reached the foyer safely. They had created the storm plan years ago, not only to keep safe, but to keep Hannah feeling calm and in charge during an emergency.

"Good job, baby girl." Brock shut the door firmly behind them. Now that they were inside the house, he could take his anxiety level down a notch.

Hannah was on the ground yanking off her wet boots and he was knocking the excess water off his cowboy hat when he heard a noise coming from the kitchen. Brock hung his hat on a hook by the door before he walked around the corner toward the sound of the noise.

"Oh!" Casey exclaimed, balancing a full glass of water in one hand and Hercules in the other. "Hey! You're back!"

"Why aren't you in the cellar?"

"The rain and the wind stopped, so I figured we were in the clear," she explained to him offhandedly on her way to greet his daughter. "You must be Hannah. I'm Casey. I've heard so much about you from my sister, Taylor." Casey smiled at the preteen who was nearly as tall as she was. "And this is the awesome Hercules."

Casey knew from her sister that Hannah was on the spectrum, so she understood when Brock's daughter didn't look her in the eye. She also knew that Hannah loved animals and it showed by the way Hannah reached over to gently pet Hercules.

"You can get acquainted in the cellar." Brock moved behind his daughter and put his hands on her shoulders. "It may look like it now, but we're not in the clear."

"No?" Casey asked him.

"No," he reiterated. "We all need to get down in the cellar. *Now.*"

For two hours, the three of them hunkered down in the cellar while the worst of the storm stalled in their region of the state. The wooden house creaked and groaned as the storm reenergized. She couldn't see it, but she had been able to hear that the force of the wind was blowing debris against the sides of the house. Casey was grateful that fate had landed her in Brock's cellar instead of being stranded out on a desolate road in a rented moving van. But her gratitude was beginning to give way to discomfort and claustrophobia. It was cool and damp down in the cellar—her skin felt clammy and she still felt chilled even after Brock gave her a blanket to wrap around her shoulders. Worse yet, the air was stuffy, and even though she had hoped she would be able to eventually ignore it, she hadn't grown accustomed to the smell at all. It was reminiscent of her middle school locker room—body odor and dirty socks.

"Do you think it's safe to go up yet?" Casey asked her host expectantly.

It had been at least fifteen minutes since the wind had knocked anything into the exterior of the house. The pounding sound that the driving rain had made as it pummeled Brock's antiquated farmhouse had died down.

"Give it a few more minutes. The last funnel touched down mighty close to here."

With a heavy sigh, Casey shifted her body to take pressure off her aching tailbone. Sitting on the floor had stopped being a fun option when she reached her thirties. She preferred a comfy couch or squishy chair. Sitting on the floor was for the birds.

"God—my poor sister. She has to be scared to death wondering where I am." Casey readjusted the blanket on her shoulders. "You know—my horoscope *did say* that this was a bad time to travel."

"You don't really believe in that, do you?" he asked her.

"Only when they're right," she said with the faintest of laughs. "I'd say a broken-down truck, a tornado and getting stuck in your smelly cellar are three very strong indicators that it was a bad time for me to travel."

She heard Brock laugh a little after she spoke, and then she realized what she had said. "That sounded really ungrateful."

"It's okay."

"I *am* grateful," she added. "I could still be out there, stuck."

"I knew what you meant," Brock reassured her.

"And now I'm babbling. If you want me to zip it, just tell me. I won't be the least bit offended. My mom has told me that I was a precocious talker and I've had the gift of gab ever since I was a toddler. Of course, Mom doesn't really mean that in the most positive of ways."

"Talking makes the time go faster," Brock reminded her.

"Well, now you're probably just being nice, but that's okay."

"I haven't been accused of that trait too often," he replied humorously.

Hannah made a content noise as she snuggled closer to her father. Ladybug, the golden Lab that Brock and Hannah called Lady for short, lifted up her head to check on Hannah before putting her head back down on her front paws. It was endearing to see the closeness between Brock and his daughter. They were so bonded that it was hard to imagine a third person in that dynamic.

Casey was sure that there were many sides of Brock that she hadn't seen—wasn't that the case with all people? But he'd been nothing but nice to her, and he was so gentle with Hannah.

"I've never seen anyone connect with Hannah as quickly as you did," Brock told her quietly.

Casey heard the admiration in his voice and it made

her feel good. "I work with kids with all sorts of disabilities for a living—I guess it's just second nature to me now."

"What do you do again? I think your sister told me once, but I apologize—I forgot."

"I wouldn't expect you to remember something like that, anyway." Casey uncrossed her legs to relieve the ache that had shifted from her tailbone to her knees. "I'm a special education teacher for Chicago public schools. I provide services for students who have individual education plans and need extra support to access the curriculum."

"Is that right?" Brock asked. "Chicago has a reputation for having some pretty rough neighborhoods, doesn't it?"

She nodded. Those rough areas were one of the main objections her father, a prominent judge in Chicago, had to her desire to become a teacher. For her mother, it was all about the prestige of the job and the money. Or lack thereof.

"I do work in a high-poverty school. It's not easy, and, yes, there are too many problems to count, but my kids make the challenges worthwhile. Most of the kids I work with—they're good kids. *Great* kids. They just need someone to care enough about them to help them succeed—to help them *supersede* their backgrounds." Casey's voice became more passionate as she continued. "Do you know that so many of the kids I serve wouldn't have needed the services of a special education teacher if they hadn't been born into poverty? They would have had the exposure to print and early literacy development, and different experiences to build background knowledge. And it's not that the parents don't *want to* provide their kids with the best start possible, but living hand-to-mouth..." Casey counted things on her fingers. "Food insecurity, illiteracy, lack of education and job opportunities, so many factors, that parents don't have the time, or the energy, or the resources to read to their children, or provide them with those vital foundational skills. By the time these kids get to kindergarten, they're already behind in all of those fundamental skills, like vocabulary and phonemic awareness... It's really sad. Shameful, really."

When Casey spoke about the kids she worked with in Chicago, her face lit up with excitement. It turned a rather ordinary face into one that was really quite extraordinary.

"You love your job."

Casey gave him a little smile that was self-effacingly saying, *What tipped you off?*

"I really appreciate your passion for your work." Brock seemed like he wanted to reassure her. To validate her. "Kids like my Hannah need teachers who are dedicated, who genuinely care about her success. You're a hero to parents like me. I mean, the way you redirected Hannah and kept her calm... It was impressive."

In the low light cast off from the lantern between them, their eyes met and held for the briefest of moments before Brock looked away. His dark hair, threaded with silver near the temple, was slicked back from his long face. His jawline was square, his brows heavy above deeply set blue eyes. When she was a scrawny teenager, and Brock was eighteen, she had thought he was *so* handsome—and she still did. But all signs of youthfulness had been worn from his face. The wrinkles on his forehead, around his mouth and eyes, were evidence of frowning and stress. This was a man who was under a major amount of pressure—she recognized the signs. She also recognized the signs of a devoted father. Whatever marital problems he was having—and she had heard from her sister that there were many—he hadn't let them interfere with his dedication to Hannah.

"Well, thank you." Casey felt her cheeks get a little warm. "I'm glad I could help."

Hercules picked that moment to sit up, stretch, yawn and then take a large leap off her thigh and onto the blanket.

"Is that a real dog? Or do you have to wind it every morning?" Brock had turned his attention to her teacup-sized poodle that had just made the large leap off her leg onto the blanket.

"*Hey!* Don't pick on Hercules!" Hannah scooped Hercules up and kissed him several times. "Though he may be but little, he is fierce!"

"Now it's getting serious. You brought Shakespeare to the table?" Brock teased her.

Hercules gave a little yap and ran around in a circle.

"A little Shakespeare never hurt anyone."

"Speak for yourself," he retorted. "I took a class on Shakespeare in college. Worst semester of my life."

"It pains me to shift the subject away from Shakespeare, because I happen to be a fan, but I think—" she nodded her head toward her pocket poodle "—he needs a bathroom break. He does have a microscopic bladder, after all—poor baby."

"Okay." Brock shook Hannah's shoulder to wake her. "I think it's safe to go topside."

Ignoring the stiffness in her joints from sitting for too long in one position, Casey stood up quickly, shed the blanket, scooped up Hercules and tucked him into the crook of her arm.

She was the caboose, and followed Brock, his daughter and their dog up to the main floor.

"Oh, wow." Casey walked to the closest window.

The storm had torn through the ranch, littering the yard with large, broken tree branches, overturned equipment and missing shingles from the roof of the barn.

"What a mess," she said to Brock.

"I'm going to check on the horses." The ranch foreman shrugged into a rain slicker. "Will you watch Hannah?"

She agreed to watch his daughter, of course. And, once both dogs had the chance to take care of business, Casey and Hannah took their canine companions back inside. It was drizzling outside, and the gray sky was so dreary, but it seemed as if the worst of the storm had finally passed them by.

"Do you have a landline, Hannah?"

Hannah showed her the phone on the other side of the refrigerator. She had periodically tried to get reception with her cell phone while they were in the cellar, without any luck. Now that they were out of the cellar, she still wasn't having any luck with reception.

Relieved to hear a dial tone when she picked up the receiver, she dialed her sister's number and silently begged her sister to answer.

"Hello?"

"Taylor! Thank goodness I got you!"

"Casey! I saw Brock's number on caller ID. I wasn't expecting to hear your voice, but I'm so glad it's you! I've been trying to get you on your cell phone for hours!"

"I knew you had to be freaking out. I'm sorry—the truck broke down, then the tornado… It's been a crazy day. How did you fare through the storm?"

"We're fine—we'll have to clean up the loose branches in the yard, but it could have been much, much worse. I'm just glad that you're okay," her sister said. "I didn't want you to drive all of my stuff here by yourself, anyway. And you said the truck broke down?"

"Small fire in the engine, yes."

"Ca-sey! I *knew* it was a bad idea!"

Casey heard the sound of her niece crying in the background. Penelope had been born premature and was prone to ear infections. She didn't say anything to her sister, but Taylor sounded exhausted.

"Tay—I wanted to do it, so I did it. I'm fine. Brock happened to show up at an opportune time, so no harm done."

There was a pause on the end of the line.

Then Taylor said, "I was wondering how you wound up with Brock."

When her sister said her brother-in-law's name, there was an underlying dislike in her tone. Casey knew from many conversations with her sister that Brock and her new husband, Clint, had a long-standing fractured relationship. From what she understood, Clint didn't like Brock any more than Brock liked him. And the only glue that bound them together was Hannah.

"He kept me safe. And he's been really nice to me."

"Well." Her sister seemed reluctant to give Brock a compliment. "That's good at least."

Casey smiled at Hannah, who was sitting at the table with an iPad while Lady took her position at Hannah's feet.

"And I've had a chance to make friends with Hannah," she said. "I hear my niece. How's she doing?"

"She's sick again." This was said with the tired voice of a first-time mother. "She hasn't slept, so I haven't slept. Clint broke his collarbone down in Laredo…"

"Oh, no, Tay—I'm so sorry to hear that."

"It couldn't be worse timing—the only upside is that he's coming home early. His best friend, Dallas, is going to drive him back and then we'll buy her a plane ticket to get her to the next stop on the circuit."

Taylor's husband was a professional bull rider; Casey didn't know how her sister, who was once married to a metrosexual man, could have wound up marrying a cowboy. But they seemed to just fit.

"He'll be home all summer then." Casey said the thought as soon as she thought it.

"That collarbone is going to be a tough one to heal, so I think he'll be out of the running this season. Maybe this will be the one that makes him rethink his career."

Still thinking about Taylor's small bungalow on the outskirts of Helena, Casey didn't respond right away. It must have clicked in Taylor's mind what she was thinking, because her sister hastened to say, "There's plenty of room here, Casey. I still want you to stay with us for the summer."

"Let's not worry about it now." Casey rubbed her temples. "First thing I need to do is find out from

Brock if the roads are even passable now so I can check on the truck. I don't think he'll mind taking me all the way into Helena if it saves you a trip."

"Call me as soon as you know the plan. Promise?"

"Of course. I love you, sis. Give Penny a kiss from me. I'll see you soon."

Casey used the restroom and then joined Hannah at the table. Hannah was looking at a large diagram of a ladybug's anatomy. Like many children diagnosed with autism, Hannah had become fixated on a topic, and that topic was ladybugs. The bathroom was decorated with ladybugs—ladybug shower curtain, ladybug toothbrush holder, ladybug towels. There was a ladybug on Hannah's shirt and Casey had spotted a ladybug backpack hanging on one of the hooks in the foyer. Their dog was named Ladybug. One of the ways she had distracted Hannah from being scared in the cellar was to redirect to conversations about ladybugs. Once Hannah got started talking about the topic that interested her most, she forgot about the storm and talked at length about the insects. Although Brock was impressed with her ability to pinpoint Hannah's interest, it wasn't rocket science. All she had to do was pay attention to observable details, which was part of her job as a special education teacher.

"What else do you have on your iPad?" she asked, curious to see Hannah's reaction.

"Stuff," Hannah replied without looking up from the screen.

Brock's daughter wasn't interested in showing her any other apps on the iPad—not in the middle of looking at ladybugs.

The door to the house swung open. Brock peeled off his wet rain slicker and tossed it onto a rocking chair just outside the front door. He stepped into the foyer, stomped his feet on the rug and slapped the rain off his hat by hitting it across his thigh a couple of times.

"How's it looking out there?" Casey asked.

Brock shook his head as he closed the front door tightly behind him. "It's a mess."

He joined them in the kitchen—it wasn't a tiny kitchen, but with Brock in it, it seemed to shrink before her eyes. He had been a tall, lanky young man the last time she had seen him. Now he was a large man, taller than most and burly. He was active and strong, but he had developed a bit of a paunch around the middle. A lumberjack. That's what he reminded her of—a Paul Bunyan lumberjack. Not many of those running around Chicago.

"I got ahold of Taylor."

Brock had just downed a glass of water and he was filling it up again. "Good. She doing okay?"

"Penny's sick again and Clint broke his collarbone, so he's heading back from Texas. She said that she weathered the storm okay, though. Just a couple of small branches in the yard. Nothing major." She noticed that Brock's demeanor didn't change at all when she mentioned that his stepbrother had gotten hurt. "What's the chance of you getting me into Helena tonight?"

"Zip." He put the empty glass on the cluttered counter. "Downed trees are blocking the major roads into town."

"You're not serious?" Casey said with a frustrated sigh. "You are serious."

"I can take you to Bent Tree or you can bunk with us tonight," Brock said. "Hannah—it's time to feed Lady. Turn off the iPad."

Hannah didn't respond.

"Hannah."

"Just one more thing." Hannah didn't look up—her entire focus was on the screen.

Brock was tired and she could see that he was losing patience.

"Here—let's do this, Hannah. I'm going to set my timer to one minute and when the timer goes off, you can turn off the iPad."

The timer on her phone was set, the one minute ran out and Hannah, albeit reluctantly, turned off the iPad and tended to Lady's needs.

Brock didn't say it with words, but there was a definite thank-you in his eyes when he looked at her.

"I don't know if I have the energy to face my aunt and uncle right now. But are you sure it would be okay if I crashed here tonight?"

"It's no problem. You can take my bed upstairs and I'll sleep on the couch."

"No—I'll take the couch."

"No—you'll take my bed. I sleep on the couch most nights, anyway."

Sleeping in a bed instead of on a couch sounded like a much better scenario. If the bed were usually empty anyway, what would it hurt to take him up on his offer?

"All right—but only if you're sure."

He didn't respond to that comment, but instead moved the conversation forward. "We'll get a good night's sleep, have breakfast and then we can stop off and check on the truck on our way to Helena."

"Oh." Casey groaned the word. "Geez. The *truck*. I hope *the Beast* is okay."

Chapter Three

By nature, she was a light sleeper. Always had been. But the night she had spent in Brock's massive California king-size bed had been one of her deepest sleeps on record. Perhaps it was the fact that she had been flat-out exhausted, or maybe it was the silky-soft material of the sheets. Either way, she had awakened from her sound sleep in the dead center of the bed, surrounded by a pile of plump pillows that had to be Brock's soon-to-be ex-wife's doing, feeling happy and content. She didn't even scramble out of bed, as was her usual practice. Instead, she opted to linger a bit, staring up at the ceiling with the comforter pulled all the way up to her nose.

"Dad says get up!" Hannah burst into the room without knocking.

Shocked out of her random, drifting thoughts, Casey

popped upright, her long auburn hair a mass of tangles. Hercules was vaulted forward, but he landed on all four paws. He waggled his tail and yapped at Hannah.

"If you want to come into someone's room, what is the polite thing to do?" Casey asked.

"Knock."

Casey gave the preteen two thumbs-up. "Okay— try it again."

"What?"

"Knocking before you come in. You knock, wait for an answer and then you come in. But only if I say it's okay. Okay?"

"Okay."

Hannah slammed the door shut, causing Hercules to yap wildly. Casey heard a knock on the door, but she waited for a couple of seconds before she answered just to make certain Hannah wouldn't burst in without getting the green light.

"Come in!"

Hannah flung open the door again with a laugh. "Breakfast!"

"Thank you, Hannah. Nice waiting, too." Casey smiled at the girl. "Can you do something for me? Would you take Hercules out to use the bathroom while I get dressed?"

Brock's daughter's face beamed at the thought of being able to carry Hercules for the first time.

"I know you'll make sure he's okay." Casey was re-assuring herself as much as she was reassuring Hannah. It was hard to let Hercules out of her sight. He was so small and vulnerable. But she had heard about Hannah's affinity for animals from Taylor, and she had seen how kind she was with her own dog, Lady.

Casey yawned several times, wiped the sleep out of her eyes and stretched her arms high above her head, before she scooted to the edge of the bed with a dramatic sigh. Rest time was officially over for her. Today, she had to go see how the Beast had fared in the storm, figure out how to get it towed if need be and then figure out whether or not she was just going to stay for a short visit with her sister and then head back to Chicago. She wanted to stay in Montana for the summer—it was too late to put in a request to work summer school. And she had been looking forward to this trip for months. She'd hate for it to all fall apart, but she couldn't imagine staying with Taylor and Clint, in their small rental, for three months. Even though Taylor would try very hard to make her feel like she wasn't a bother, she knew that she would, in fact, be an intrusion on the newlyweds.

Casey went into the tiny attached bathroom to fix her hair, if possible, and wash her mouth out with mouthwash. When she got a load of herself in the mirror, she started to laugh. She looked like a redheaded Medusa. She had tried to tame her hair before bed, but it hadn't worked. Now, it was even worse after a night of sleep.

"Whatever." Casey made a face.

She took off the white undershirt Brock had let her borrow. After getting dressed, she made the bed, and then left the folded undershirt on the comforter, along with the pajama bottoms she hadn't used. Brock's pajama bottoms had just slipped right down her hips.

Finally, she retrieved her beloved Jimmy Choo boots from beneath a nearby chair and stared at them sadly. They were ruined. Her beautiful, *expensive*, Jimmy

Choo boots that she had vision-boarded for months, that she had saved a little every month to buy, were caked with red clay and still wet from the day before.

"You poor, poor boots. You didn't deserve this. *I* didn't deserve this." Today, she wasn't even going to try to be careful with them. There was no use shutting the gate *after* the cow got out. Resigned to their untimely demise, Casey shoved her feet into the boots and headed downstairs.

"Good morning." Casey was met with a cornucopia of breakfast food smells when she entered the kitchen.

"Mornin'," her host greeted her. "Coffee's hot, mugs in the drying rack are a safe bet."

"Bless you." Casey poured herself a cup of coffee.

"If you need milk or sugar, they're somewhere in the fridge. Just fish around."

"I take it black." She took her coffee to the table.

Brock was manning the stove in a "Kiss the Chef" apron, while Hannah, who had already had her breakfast, was on the floor formally introducing Lady and Hercules in the light of day. They had met informally in the cellar, but this was the first time that they were nose to nose, so to speak. Lady was lying down on the floor, her head between her two outstretched front legs, obviously trying to do her best to make friends, while Hercules was yapping as loudly and as ferociously as he could manage in order to assert his dominance in the relationship.

"Hercules—that's not nice."

"How do you take your eggs?" Brock asked her.

"Are they eggs from free-range chickens?"

"The chickens live out back. Is that free enough for you?"

"Lucy and Ethel!" Hannah supplied the names of the chickens.

"*I Love Lucy* and ladybugs. That's what she loves." Brock looked over at his daughter.

"And animals," Casey added.

Brock turned his body away from the stove and toward Casey. This wasn't the first time he'd wanted to get a better look at her in his favorite shirt. It engulfed her, but it looked good on her. Her hair, seemingly more red than auburn in the daylight, was mussed and wild, and he could swear that she had the brightest green eyes he'd ever seen on a woman.

"And animals," he echoed her sentiment. Then, so he wouldn't be standing in his kitchen ogling her like a teenage boy, he asked again, "How do you take your eggs?"

"Scrambled works."

"How about some bacon made from free-range pigs?" Brock teased her.

"No. Thank you. I'm a pescatarian."

Brock wasn't exactly sure he'd heard her right, so after he got the eggs cooking, he turned back around.

"Did you say you were a Presbyterian?"

"No!" Casey laughed so easily. It had been a long time since he'd heard a woman laughing in his house. "Pescatarian. I don't eat meat, except for fish. But I'm trying to give up fish, too."

"What for?"

She smiled at him; she had deep dimples in each of her pale cheeks. Sweet.

"Health mainly—bacon is full of fat and salt. High in cholesterol." Casey wrinkled her nose at the thought of eating bacon.

"Dad has high cholesterol and high blood pressure," Hannah shouted from the living room.

"Hannah—remember what we said about private information?"

"But Dr. Patel says that he has the heart of a much younger man."

It was too late to cork that bottle—instead, Brock decided to ignore the fact that his daughter had just provided a near stranger with all of the recent results of his physical and finish scrambling the eggs. The only thing that she hadn't shared, because she hadn't been in the room to hear it, was the fact that he had a mildly enlarged prostate and needed to drop twenty pounds.

Brock put a healthy portion of scrambled eggs on the plate, along with cheese grits and a couple of biscuits.

"Eat it while it's hot." He put the plate down in front of her and then sat down on the opposite side of the kitchen table.

"Mmm. Thank you. I'm so hungry." Casey stabbed a couple of eggs with her fork. "What about you?"

"I ate hours ago. We've been waiting on you."

Casey chewed her eggs quickly so she could ask, "Why didn't you wake me up when you got up?"

"I got up while it was still dark."

"Oh." That was different. "Well, why didn't you get me up sooner, then?"

"No harm done. It's my day off and I'm not looking forward to getting up on the roof to see how many shingles need to be replaced. You need salt or pepper for the eggs?"

"No. I'm good. These eggs are delicious, FYI."

"That's good."

She finished her breakfast, offered to clean the dishes, which he refused, and then all five of them, two dogs and three humans, piled into Brock's truck. First stop was the moving truck and the second stop was Taylor's house.

"I feel really bad about Clint breaking his collarbone."

She watched Brock's face for a reaction. There wasn't one.

"He was supposed to be gone all summer," she added.

Brock glanced over at his passenger. She had been biting her lip nervously since they had gotten into the truck. Now he understood some of her nerves at least— she was worried about living in a house with a newly married couple and a newborn. Even if they told her that she wasn't going to be a bother, Brock had a feeling that Casey wouldn't even take the chance of being an inconvenience to anybody. During the short time they had spent together, she was always worried about his comfort and his feelings, as well as the comfort and feelings of his daughter. He found her politeness refreshing.

"Might be mighty tight over at their place," Brock said, broaching the topic.

Casey turned her head his way, met him eye to eye. She said, "I was thinking the exact same thing."

"You thinking about cutting your trip short?"

The woman beside him breathed in very deeply and then let it out on a long, extended sigh. "I'd hate to do that. But I just might have to…"

"It'd be a shame. Coming all this way just to go home."

Out of the corner of his eye, he noticed Casey making little circles on the top of Hercules's head. "I know.

But I can't impose on Taylor for the summer—not now. Newlyweds need their private time. Besides, Clint is hurt. He's not going to be in any mood to have a houseguest."

"That's right," he agreed, then added, "I have a loft apartment above the barn. It's a little rough, but it's livable."

Casey looked at Brock, interested.

"The way you are with Hannah—like I said last night—it's impressive. And it got me thinking that we could help each other out. Hannah does fine with academics—she's even strong in math and science. But it's her…"

"Pragmatics," she filled in for him.

He glanced at her again. "Exactly. As you can tell from our breakfast conversation, there's still a bit of a ways to go with that."

Casey nodded her agreement—a deficit with social use of language was a universal symptom of individuals with autism across the spectrum.

"How 'bout I let you use the loft for the summer in exchange for some private social language support. How does that set with you?"

Casey stared at Brock's profile. "Are you serious?"

"Yeah. Why? Do you think it's a bad idea?"

"Heck, no, I don't think it's a bad idea. I think it's a pretty genius idea," she said with a smile. "Can I let you know?"

"Sure. Offer stands."

Casey's smile was short-lived.

"Oh! No, no, no, no, no, no, no, no, *no*!" She put her hands on top of her head in disbelief.

The rental truck was knocked on its side.

"What's wrong?" Hannah looked up from her iPad.

Brock pulled onto the berm on the opposite side of the road from the rental truck.

"Damn."

"Swear jar!" Hannah yelled.

"Hannah," Casey said in a stunned, monotone voice. "Would you hold Hercules for me?"

"Stay in the truck and wait for us, okay, baby girl?" Brock pulled his hat off the dash and pushed it onto his head.

Together, they crossed the road. In silence, they both walked around the perimeter of the truck. The back was still locked, but the truck was facing the wrong direction.

"The only thing I can figure is that a twister caught it and spun it ninety degrees. Then for kicks, knocked it on its side."

Casey stood, shaking her head back and forth, and back and forth. She couldn't find words. Everything her sister owned, everything her sister cherished, was in that truck. There was a collection of Royal Doulton statues worth thousands, as well as a collection of Lladró figurines, also worth thousands. Taylor had been collecting them since she was a teenager.

"I want to cry," Casey said quietly. "I really do."

Brock looked down at her, she saw him in her periphery, and then he took his cell phone out of his pocket and made a phone call. She heard him make arrangements with a friend who had a tow truck made to haul big rigs to come and set the Beast upright and tow it to Helena.

"Thank goodness I took the insurance." Casey couldn't stop staring at the rental truck. She'd never seen one from this angle before. It was a bit like looking at a surrealist painting, trying to figure out why people were walking on the ceiling.

"Right?" Brock crossed his arms in front of his body. "My friend Billy will be able to get this right-side up sometime around noon."

"Thank you."

They stood together, both looking at the truck without anything else to say about it.

"Are you done looking at it?" the ranch foreman asked her.

Casey sighed. "Yeah. I guess. The damage is done."

"That's right."

The rest of the way into Helena, Casey felt sick to her stomach. Taylor was going to be heartbroken and it was her fault. She was the one who'd had the idea of saving her sister some cash by renting a truck and driving it herself. Taylor had said, repeatedly, that she thought it was best if professional movers brought her things to Montana. But, as she always did, she persisted until she wore Taylor down. And now, all of her belongings were trapped in a toppled rental truck on the side of a desolate Montana highway. Brilliant.

"This is it." Brock stopped at the end of the driveway of a little Craftsman bungalow.

With a heavy sigh, Casey nodded her head. "Yep."

"Can I go in and see Penny?" Hannah asked excitedly.

Casey met Brock's eye before she said, "Not this time, Hannah. Penny has an ear infection."

"Next time," Brock added. "I'll call you as soon as I hear something from Billy."

"Text me if I don't answer."

"Consider it done."

She stood with the truck door open and mustered a small smile for him. "Thank you for everything, Brock. Seriously. Above and beyond the call of duty."

He tipped his hat to her, and she interpreted that gesture as a *you're welcome* and a *thank you, too*. She got out of the truck and said goodbye to Hannah and her father.

Her sister was opening the door at the same time Brock was pulling away.

"Casey!" Taylor was holding her baby daughter in her arms.

They embraced tightly, as they always did. They were more than sisters—they were, and always had been, best friends.

"Oh, Tay—she's even prettier in person." Casey touched Penelope's creamy, chubby cheek. "Hi, Penny, you sweet, sweet thing. Your aunt Casey is going to spoil you *absolutely* rotten! Yes, I am!"

"She's so fussy right now because she doesn't feel well." Taylor kissed her daughter's warm forehead.

"Poor Penny." Casey looked at her little niece compassionately.

"I'm so happy to see you, Casey." Taylor hugged her again. "I've missed you like crazy."

Together they walked up the driveway to the front door of the bungalow. "I've missed you. I hate that we don't live in the same town anymore."

"Me, too." Taylor shut the front door behind them. "Let me see if she'll lie down for her nap. It'll give us a chance to catch up. She hasn't slept well for a couple of days, so cross your fingers."

Casey held up her crossed fingers for her sister to see.

Taylor didn't reappear for a while. When her sister returned to the living room, she was talking in a quieter voice.

"Okay—she's down. For how long is debatable! Is it too early for wine?"

"No. Bring it on, sis." She could use a large glass or two.

Taylor had been diagnosed with the inability to lactate after the birth of her daughter, and the only upside her sister could find was the fact that she had been cleared to drink wine.

Casey sat down at the breakfast bar while her sister got the wineglasses.

"Red or white?" Taylor asked her from the open refrigerator.

"Either—as long as it's not too dry."

Taylor held up a bottle for her to see. "How about this?"

Casey gave her the "okay" sign; generous portions of wine were poured and the two of them moved to the cozy family room next to the kitchen. Taylor immediately coaxed Hercules onto her lap, and the micropoodle didn't hesitate to abandon her owner for a novel lap.

"Traitor," Casey said to her canine companion.

"Here's to a great summer." Taylor touched her glass to hers.

"To a great summer." She took several large gulps of the wine. Taylor hadn't even asked her about the rental truck.

Her sister curled her legs to the side, leaned into the couch cushion and smiled happily at her. "I am so happy to see you."

"You may not feel that way in a minute."

Taylor's eyebrows dropped and her pretty blue eyes registered confusion. "What are you talking about?"

Casey downed the rest of her wine. One of her most intense childhood memories was the time that she decapitated Taylor's favorite Barbie doll and then flushed the head just to see if it would indeed flush. It had. And Taylor had gone absolutely crazy-town ballistic on her and then stopped speaking to her for a month. Granted, they were kids when that happened. But then again, this was much worse than decapitating Barbie. *Much* worse.

Chapter Four

Her sister's reaction to the news that her belongings were trapped in a tipped-over truck on the side of the road was not at all what she had anticipated. Taylor wasn't angry. Taylor wasn't looking to blame her. Instead, her sister was simply grateful that Casey and Hercules were okay. Taylor had always had a flair for the dramatic, and this change in her was unexpected, but it was a change for the better. Perhaps it was the fact that she was a mother now; or perhaps it was because she had already lost one of the most valuable gifts she had ever been given—Penelope's twin brother, Michael, had died soon after he was born. Casey hadn't experienced it, but she didn't have to experience something to understand that losing a child, an infant, could change a person forever.

"Are you sure you don't want to stay with us? Clint

and I both *want* you to stay," Taylor asked her as they walked together along the brick walkway that led to the driveway.

She'd been in Montana for a week already, and so much had happened: the Beast had been towed into town, her travel trunk and Taylor's boxes had been recovered and Clint had arrived home with his arm in a sling and loaded up on pain medication. According to the doctors in Texas, Clint's healing time would be roughly a month or two, but he wouldn't be fit to get back on a bull. He was grounded for the entire summer, at least.

Casey, who was holding her niece in her arms, was too busy nuzzling Penny's sweet-smelling neck to pay full attention to her sister. "Mmm, you have that new baby smell, Penny." She hugged her niece, not wanting to let her go. Casey smiled at her sister. "Babies! They always smell so *good*. I wish I could bottle this smell and take it with me."

"Casey! Please, stop ignoring me. You came all the way to Montana to be with Penny and me, and I feel like *deep down inside* you think that we don't want you here because Clint is home. And that's not the case at all."

Casey smooched her niece all over her face one last time before she said, "Trade."

Taylor frowned at her as they traded babies—her sister handed over Hercules and she handed over Penny.

"I don't think you're kicking me out, Tay. I know you want me to stay. I know Clint is sincere when he says that he'll be happy to have me staying on his couch for three months, but I'm telling you, it's gonna wear real thin by the end of four weeks. Trust me. He's an active guy and now he's stuck with his arm in a sling when he should be out earning points. Your husband is going to want to sit on his couch and watch TV, in his tighty-whities, whenever the mood strikes."

Her sister didn't respond for a second or two, because Taylor knew she was right.

"I'll come and visit all the time. I'll be here on a moment's notice if you need me. Nothing's changed."

For the last week, her sister had been debating her choice to stay in Brock's loft apartment with her. Taylor had her own agenda: she either wanted her to stay with her *or* stay with their aunt Barb and uncle Hank at Bent Tree Ranch. Basically, anywhere besides Brock's ranch.

Taylor's eyes had a watery sheen and Casey knew that her sister was upset to see her go. "Look—I know you don't like the idea that I took Brock up on his offer, but it really is for the best. His place is closer to Helena than Bent Tree. And I love the idea of being able to ride anytime I want. Brock says he has a palomino mare who's getting barn sour. I'm actually going to be doing *him* a favor by riding her this summer."

Her sister wiped under her left eye with her pinky. "I know how much you want to ride again."

This was Taylor's way of giving in to the inevitable.

"Come here and give me another hug." Casey hugged her sister again, and then kissed baby Penelope's chubby hand.

"I want one," she told her sister of her niece.

"It's the best hard work I've ever done," said Taylor.

Casey opened the door to the light blue vintage VW Bug sitting in the driveway. She paused before getting in the driver's seat.

"And Taylor...I'm perfectly ready to like your husband very much."

Taylor beamed at her with pleasure. "He's a good one, right?"

Casey nodded as she got into the blue Bug and then put Hercules in his new, less fancy dog carrier for safe traveling. She put the key in the ignition, cranked the engine, then rolled down the window.

"Thanks for loaning me your car, Tay."

After her divorce, Taylor had sold her BMW, left her executive job at the bank, put her stuff in storage and then drove this very Bug from Chicago to Montana. It was on that trip, a trip where she had ridden a portion of the Continental Divide Trail on horseback, that she met her husband, Clint.

"Now you won't be stuck," Taylor said to her. "That car brought me a lot of luck. Maybe it will be lucky for you, too."

Casey backed out of the driveway with a sense of anticipation and excitement that was making her stomach feel a bit queasy. It felt as if she were heading off to her own adventure, much like her sister had last year. She waved her hand, tooted the horn and shouted one last "I love you" to her sister and niece before Casey set her course for Brock McAllister's ranch. She had the distinct feeling that this summer was going to be one of the best summers of her life. And she couldn't wait for it to start!

Casey slowed her speed in order to take the bumps in the dirt and gravel drive to Brock's ranch. The heavy rain from the storm had deepened the potholes, which made it difficult to navigate in the VW bug. Brock, she noticed, had already gone a long way toward clearing the debris; stacks of large branches dotted the side of the road every hundred feet or so. As the house came into view, Casey had the strangest feeling in her gut. She felt like she *belonged* there. Whatever lingering doubt she had in her mind about her choice to stay in Brock's barn loft studio apartment vanished. She was in the right place, at the right time, and doing exactly what she was meant to do.

Brock was on the roof repairing shingles when he heard the distinctive sound of an old school VW coming up the drive.

Casey.

He stood upright, wiped the sweat off his neck with the bandana from his back pocket and then stared at the end of the driveway, waiting to catch the first glimpse of Casey as she arrived. He had seen her once over the last week, briefly, when he had picked up her trunk from her sister's house and brought it back to the ranch. He didn't understand it, really, but he had actually missed her. He had *missed* her. And, perhaps even more important, Hannah had missed her, too.

He waved his hand in the air so she would see him. At the same time Casey was waving her hand out the driver's window, Brock heard the slam of the screen door and the pounding of his daughter's feet on the wood planks of the porch. Hannah had been hyped up all day in anticipation of Casey's arrival. Right behind Hannah was Lady, barking and wagging her tail.

Normally, he didn't like to have a job interrupted once he started, but now seemed like a good time to take a break. He climbed down the ladder and followed his daughter and dog to where Casey had parked her car.

"Don't strangle her, Hannah." Brock laughed at how tightly Hannah was hugging Casey around the neck.

Brock watched as Casey made a fuss over his daughter, and then squatted down to hug Lady. A flush of excitement and happiness had turned her pale skin a pretty shade of light pink. In the sunlight, the reddish freckles on her face and the red of her thick hair pulled back into a ponytail were so striking. And then there were her eyes. So wide and so green—he always had to remind himself not to stare.

"You've really put a dent in it!" Casey said about the progress he had made with the cleanup.

"I've been hammering away at it. Little by little." Brock was glad that it was his turn to greet Casey.

She smiled at him with that open, friendly smile of hers. It had been an awfully long time since a woman had smiled at him like that—no reservation, no pretense or judgment, just open and friendly. That smile was a magnet for him and he realized that now—by the simple fact that he was standing down here instead of still working up on the roof.

"Do you want to start getting settled in?"

"Absolutely." Casey walked around to the passenger side and got Hercules.

Hannah was running like a wild child around in circles, her long, tangled curls flying behind her.

"She's been like this all morning," Brock explained. "Usually the medications keep the hyperactivity in check enough for her to function, but not on days like today, when she's excited about something."

"I understand," Casey reassured him.

That's when it really sunk in—he didn't have to explain or justify or apologize for his daughter's behavior. Casey worked with children with disabilities for a living—she, more than anyone else in his life, would truly understand Hannah. It was a relief to spend time with someone who could understand, and accept, his daughter for who she was, regardless of her behavior—good, bad or indifferent.

"I did warn you that it's humble," Brock said as they reached the top of the stairs that lead to the loft apartment above the barn.

"I'll spruce it up." Casey didn't mind humble. And, if it was dirty, there usually wasn't much that couldn't be fixed with elbow grease. She'd never been afraid of hard work or of getting dirty.

Brock opened the door and let her go in first. He was right—the loft apartment with its pitched roof and rough-hewn, wide-planked wooden floor was indeed humble. But the inside of the roof was lined with sweet-smelling cedar, and there was a single bed in one corner of the room, and a small love seat on the other side. The bathroom was tiny and the kitchen only accommodated a hot plate, microwave and little refrigerator. Her large black trunk, a trunk her mother had used when she went to boarding school, was waiting for her at the end of the bed.

Brock had to duck his head as to not bump on the low part of the ceiling—he could only stand completely upright when he was standing directly beneath the pitched ceiling.

"I tried to straighten up the place a bit." To her ears, he sounded a little self-conscious.

"This is great." Casey wanted to reassure him. "It's perfect for us."

She saw a faint smile move across his face. He was pleased that she was pleased.

"Well, I'll let you settle into the place. I've got more work to get done before supper," Brock said, his head bent down so he didn't bang it on the top of the door frame. "You can use the kitchen for cooking—the hot plate is only good for so much. And you're always welcome to join us for meals."

"Thank you—let's just play it by ear, see how it goes."

Brock nodded his agreement before he ducked his head completely free of the door frame, put his hat back on his head and then left her to her own devices.

The first thing she did in her new home was let Hercules out of his carrier so he could get used to the smells and layout of the loft. Next she checked the bathroom accommodations and the feel of the mattress, before she unlocked the trunk and began to unpack. Every now and again, she would look out the window and watch Brock at his work. He was focused and relentless in the way he attacked his work—that kind of work ethic was attractive to her. It reminded her of the work ethic that her own father and grandfather had both had.

It didn't take long for her to get settled into her summer loft apartment. Hercules had his toys strewn across the floor, which made her feel right at home. She scooped up her poodle and sat on the bed to contemplate her next move: to take a nap, or not to take a nap—that was the dilemma. In the end, the "take a nap" side won out. She kicked off her boots and curled up on her side. The bed was just big enough for her and Hercules.

"Mmm." Casey closed her eyes with a contented sigh.

She had managed to find the perfect spot to spend a stress-free, worry-free summer. She usually worked during the summer session—this was her first real summer off since she had graduated with her master's degree in special education and took a job with the public school system.

She was in a comfortable bed, the cedar on the roof smelled sweet and there was a gentle breeze coming in through the open window. Life was, indeed, pretty darn good.

Casey had dozed off quickly and was awakened abruptly. Hannah burst through the door; the door swung open and hit the wall with a loud thud. Casey sprung upright, catapulting poor Hercules forward.

"My stars, Hannah!" She clutched the material above her rapidly beating heart. "You scared me! Remind me again about what you should do before you come into a room?"

Hannah spun around in the center of her bedroom/living room combo space, her head tilted back and her arms spread out wide like airplane wings.

"I was supposed to knock." The girl kept on spinning. "Dad wants to know if you want to have some gluten-free mac and cheese with us."

Casey felt a little foggy brained; she rubbed the sleep out of her eyes, then blinked several times to get a clearer view of the preteen spinning like a top.

"Tell your dad I'll be down in a minute."

Hannah left as quickly as she came, without a greeting or a salutation. There was a lot of work to be done to improve Hannah's social language skills. It would just take time and patience. But the reality was, and she hoped Brock was realistic about it, Hannah was never going to have completely "normal" pragmatic skills; it was possible, however, for Hannah to have friends, a job and a fulfilling social life. With supportive people in her life, Hannah's quirks and slightly askew social skills would be expected, understood and accepted.

Casey freshened up a bit and then headed down to the farmhouse. As expected, Brock was at the stove with his standard "Kiss the Chef" apron on, which may have been feminizing on some men, but not on the ranch foreman. Hannah was at the table eating macaroni and cheese out of her plastic ladybug bowl, with her ladybug silverware. Casey had a feeling that Hannah insisted on eating out of that particular bowl, using those particular utensils—and if she didn't get her way, she would either begin to have a tantrum or flat-out refuse to eat.

"Thanks for the invite." Casey sat down at the table.

"It's gluten free." Brock handed her a bowl. "Hannah's allergic."

"I figured." Casey nodded. "I actually dated someone who had celiac disease, so I have a lot of gluten-free recipes stored on my phone if you want to see if I have any that you don't have."

"That would help," Brock told her. "I have a heck of a time getting her to eat much of anything other than mac and cheese. That's all she wants. Mac and cheese."

"I have some tricks up my sleeve," Casey reassured him.

Hannah finished her meal quickly, left the table

without taking her bowl to the sink and ended up on the floor in the living room playing with Hercules.

"I'd like to take a couple of days to get settled in here, let Hannah get used to the change, and in the meantime, we can sit down and talk about some practical goals," Casey said quietly.

Brock agreed with her timeline. Any change, even if it were a positive change like Casey coming to stay on the ranch for the summer, would be difficult for Hannah to process.

"I'd like to hear your thoughts." Brock stabbed a chunk of hot dog he had mixed into his mac and cheese with his fork. Before he took that bite he added, "I'm sure you have some."

He was right—she did. Her brain just naturally observed children with special needs, catalogued the behaviors to try to fit the pieces into a puzzle and then, always, there were a list of goals that emerged from her informal, naturalistic evaluation. She had been a special education teacher for a decade and it was like breathing now—it happened without thinking about it. And, in the short time she had observed Hannah, she had made a laundry list of pragmatic goals—but it was always up to the parent and child, if possible, to help prioritize those goals.

"This arrangement is going to work out real well for all of us," Brock interrupted her thoughts.

She looked up from her bowl—she had been staring at it, but her thoughts were on Hannah. "I think so, too."

After they were done with their food, they lingered at the table for a little while longer, making small talk mainly, before clearing the table. Casey offered to wash the dishes, but Brock told her to just pile them in the sink and he'd get around to them later. The outside of the house was where Brock liked to spend his time and energy—that was obvious by how far along in the cleanup outside he was. On the other hand, the inside of the house was as messy or even more messy than it had been a week ago. For Hannah's sake especially, some semblance of order and cleanliness needed to be established in the house. She wasn't going to lead with that thought—Brock might not appreciate her butting in that far to his personal space. Yet if she was going to earn her keep, she had to be honest with him. Part of her job had always been to have courageous conversations with parents.

"Good morning!" Casey greeted him with that bright smile that lit up her impish face.

"Howdy." He was surprised to see her up so early and said as much.

Casey fell in beside him and walked to the barn with him.

"I'm an early riser," she explained. "The other day was an anomaly. Can I help?"

He had gotten Hannah started with her morning routine and now he was going to move rapidly through his morning barn routine before heading over to Bent Tree Ranch for the day. He had been working at Bent Tree since he was a teen, and had managed to work his way to ranch foreman. It was a big job for a big ranch and he took his role seriously. And even though Hank Brand, Casey's uncle, gave him a lot of latitude and a flexible schedule, he didn't want to ever have it appear that he was taking advantage of his goodwill.

"I wouldn't mind a hand," he told her.

His new tenant was dressed for the barn in slim-fitting faded jeans, ankle-high paddock boots and an untucked Kelly green T-shirt.

"You mind mucking?" Brock led the way into the feed room.

"Don't think I'm weird—but I actually enjoy mucking out stalls." She took the pitchfork from him. "I always say that I have to be from good peasant stock because I'd much rather be mucking out stalls than sitting in an office somewhere. When I sweat, I actually feel like I accomplished something."

Brock easily hoisted a bale of hay onto his left shoulder. "I already think you're a little weird."

Caught off guard by Brock's rare show of humor, Casey had a delayed response. "I'll take that as a compliment."

Brock didn't turn around—he kept on walking down the concrete breezeway of the barn. But he did say, "It was meant as one."

Casey happily mucked out the six stalls in the barn and made the acquaintance of all the horses stabled there, as well as Lucy and Ethel, the free-range chickens. When she finished with the chore, she was winded and her shoulders were aching, but she felt proud of herself. She had ridden since she was a kid and she had competed in dressage nationally; when she went to college, her horses were sold and she hadn't had much of an opportunity to ride since. This was her chance to get back into a sport she loved. It felt so good to be back in a barn.

Chapter Five

"How'd we fare?" Brock had hay all over the front of his shirt and stuck to the side of his thick, ruddy neck. The man was truly built like a brick house—his muscles were thick, heavy and rounded—defined like a body builder or someone who worked out in the gym. She leaned the pitchfork against one of the walls and gave him a thumbs-up.

"He's amazing." Casey walked over to where Brock was standing.

A plate on the stall read "The Mighty Taj." The way Brock was petting and talking to Taj, she could tell how much he loved this big beauty of a horse.

"Is he a Friesian?" She reached out to pet the silkiest part of his nose—right between the two flaring nostrils.

"That he is," Brock said with pride in his voice.

"I've never seen one in person. Only in the movies—almost every black horse I see in a movie is a Friesian."

Brock rubbed Taj on the neck and then gave him a hard couple of pats with words of affection. And then he asked her, "What did you think of the palomino?"

"She's a sweetheart—and so pretty," she said happily.

Good as Gold, Gigi for short, was a stocky, twelve-year-old quarter horse mare that was to be her horse for the summer.

"I can tell that she's developed some bad habits, but nothing that can't be remediated with time. Thank you for letting me work with her this summer. It's really a dream come true for me."

"It's good for both of us. I don't have time to work with her. If you weren't here to work with her, I'd have to think about finding her a new home. It's not fair not to work her out regularly."

"Well, it means a lot to me. I've wanted to get back into horses for years, but it's expensive. And even though I love my job—and I do—it's just good that I'm not in it for the money."

"I remember you were a good rider," Brock said to her, their eyes meeting and holding for a minute or two. "I remember that about you."

She remembered so much about Brock—a young man who seemed to have disappeared completely. What a crush she had had on *that* Brock! She'd pined for him as only a teenage girl can pine—and the fact that he'd been engaged to Shannon, a beauty pageant winner, had been a knife in her tender teenage heart.

He was different now. It made her wonder—where had the old Brock McAllister gone?

"I'm going to get Hannah ready to go. I'll be at Bent Tree all day. Are you going to be visiting your aunt and uncle today?"

Good question. She had been in stealth mode, avoiding her extended family. Not because she *didn't* want to see them—she did—she had just wanted to do it on her own terms, when she was a little bit more rested.

She frowned in thought. Her preference was to start working with Gigi. But she had been in Montana for a little over a week without visiting her aunt and uncle—if she waited any longer she was heading into "hurt feelings" territory.

"I probably should." It was a statement that sounded a bit like a question.

"You probably should," he agreed with her without hesitation.

Oh, all right. Fine!

"I'll call Aunt Barb now," she told him.

"She'll be glad to hear from you." Brock started to head back to the house. "I saved some pancakes for you. Just nuke 'em if you want 'em."

Casey thanked him while she waited for her aunt to pick up the phone.

"Hello?"

"Aunt Barb? It's your wayward niece, Casey."

"Casey-face? I've been waiting all week for a phone call from you! What in the world took you so long?"

She wasn't too long into the conversation with her aunt before they made arrangements for her to have lunch at Bent Tree; it wasn't her first choice, but sometimes with family, you had to put off what you wanted to do in order to do the right thing.

Darn it!

* * *

"*Oh*, Casey! Give me a hug!" Aunt Barb greeted her as she always had, with a big smile on her face, warmth in her striking blue eyes and a genuine hug filled with love and welcome.

"Hi, Aunt Barb." Casey hugged her aunt tightly. "I'm sorry I didn't call right away."

Aunt Barb nodded her head. "I was very upset with you. I couldn't understand why you didn't call us when you ran into trouble with the truck—when you needed a place to stay. Do you want some coffee? I just put a fresh pot on."

Casey declined the coffee—she had already had two cups of Brock's personal high-octane morning blend. She followed her aunt into what had always been one of her favorite rooms in Bent Tree's main farmhouse—the study. The walls of the study were lined floor to ceiling with bookshelves jam-packed full of books. There was also a large hearth where her aunt hung stockings during Christmastime. Coming to Montana, to the ranch where her father had been raised, had always been magical for her. So many wonderful family memories were tied to this home, to this land—to the people of Bent Tree. And then, after her grandfather Brand's last will and testament was read, the family imploded and nothing was ever the same. Her father stopped speaking to his brother, her uncle Hank. Family vacations to the ranch ended. She still felt a little awkward being at Bent Tree now. Perhaps that's why she had put off coming. This was her first time back to the ranch since she was a teen. And somehow, even though her father knew she would be visiting the ranch, it felt like a betrayal.

"Is it okay if I let Hercules out?"

"Who?" Her aunt tossed some pillows out of her way so she could sit in her usual spot.

Casey held up the carrier that resembled an over-size purse. "Hercules, the greatest dog that ever was or will be."

Aunt Barb was an avid animal lover. The minute she realized that Casey had a friend she immediately changed course and, instead of sitting down, came over to say hello.

Hercules was let out of the carrier and into Aunt Barb's hands. "You are too cute. Is he a toy or a teacup?"

"He's a teacup—a micro-teacup, actually. I adopted him from the poodle rescue. My tiny apartment could only really handle a tiny dog."

"Well, you want to stay with your auntie for a while, don't you, Hercules? We had to put Ilsa down last month—it's been so strange without her in the house."

"Oh. I'm so sorry to hear that." She remembered playing with Ilsa, the family's German shepherd, when Ilsa was just a puppy.

"Thank you. Your uncle's been having the toughest time with it. They get in your heart, don't they?"

With Hercules in her lap, her aunt sat down, then Casey sat down across from her on the couch so they could talk easily.

"It's been such a long time, Casey." Her aunt looked at her with sorrow in her eyes. "So much time has passed. I don't want to dwell on what we can't change— what would be the sense in that?—but I have to say this. You do know that we always wanted to see you— you and your sister were always welcome."

This was the topic that made Casey squirm inside.

This "feud" had started between brothers, but it had impacted everyone. Taylor and she hadn't had a vote—their aunt, uncle and cousins were taken away from them without warning or discussion. When Taylor made the decision to return to the ranch last year, she blazed a trail for Casey's return. But she still didn't feel comfortable talking about it.

"I know, Aunt Barb."

"Well." Her aunt's hands were busy petting Hercules. "You're here now. That's what matters."

She *was* here now. The smells of the house, the sounds of the house, seemed to be a part of the very core of who she was now. Everything—*everything*—unlocked memories and brought them to the forefront of her mind. Things that she hadn't thought about in years—like the way the library always smelled a little soapy and clean because of the leather cleaner her aunt used to care for the furniture. And the way the wide wooden planks in the hallway creaked across from a grandmother clock that always ran fifteen minutes fast. It was…overwhelming.

They caught up for a while and then they moved to the kitchen for lunch. Uncle Hank made it a point to stop his work and drive back to the main house to join them. It was so strange seeing her aunt and uncle in person. Their images had stayed frozen in her mind—and even though she had seen pictures of them on social media, it was different seeing them in person. Uncle Hank, a tall, slender man with deeply tanned skin, deep-set blue eyes and white hair that he always parted on the left and combed neatly back from his narrow face, was still a handsome man—but he looked so old to her. And Aunt Barb, who was from Chicago

and had worked hard to maintain her city chic in spite
of the fact that she had lived on a cattle ranch for over
forty years, had aged gracefully. But even though she
still wore her hair pulled back in a neat-as-a-pin chi-
gnon, it wasn't blond any longer—it was silver. Time
had moved on, had changed them all, and it made her
acutely aware of everything she had missed.

"How's Brock been treatin' you over there at his
place?" Uncle Hank asked her between bites of his
baked chicken breast that he had smothered with homemade barbeque sauce.

"I already told her that she should be staying with
us. We've got plenty of room upstairs." Aunt Barb sent
her a disapproving glance.

"He's been so good to me," she told her uncle.

"He's a good man," Uncle Hank said simply, but
Casey knew how much weight that simple compliment carried. Her uncle wasn't an easy man to impress.

Hank turned in his chair to look at his wife, who
was opening the oven. "Are you joining us, Barb?
We're almost done here."

"I'm coming, I'm coming." Aunt Barb brought a
plate of corn bread hot out of the oven and then took
her place at the table.

"I appreciate the offer to stay here, Aunt Barb." Casey
took a piece of corn bread and slathered it with butter.
"But I really wanted to be closer to town. And I like that
the loft is my own little private retreat from the world."
Casey poured honey all over her corn bread. "Besides,
Brock's place is halfway between Bent Tree and Helena—I'm close to everyone there."

"Well." Aunt Barb's tone reflected her continued

dissatisfaction with the arrangement. "Now that you know the way, I'm sure you'll want to come to Bent Tree for regular visits."

Aunt Barb was happy to dog-sit Hercules while Casey visited the horses in the main barn on her way to see the chapel. The chapel, a one-hundred-year-old structure, had been built by her great-great-grandfather and had been moved down the mountain so that it could be restored and enjoyed by new generations of Brands for decades to come. Her memories of the chapel were seared into her mind. She couldn't wait to see the restored structure in person—she imagined that the pictures she had seen couldn't truly do it justice.

Casey took her time in the barn, personally greeting each horse and putting little pieces of apple and carrot in their food buckets as treats. So far, it had been a successful trip back to Bent Tree. She couldn't believe that she had been worried about opening her life to this part of her family. Yes, her father still refused to speak to Hank, but she was a grown woman. Ultimately, she had to decide who she let into her life.

"Heads up!"

Casey had been in her own world, deep in thought, when the loudly shouted warning shocked her back to the present. An early model pickup truck had been backed into an open part of the barn and there was a young man in his twenties preparing to throw a bale of hay in her direction.

"Did I scare ya?" The young man stood upright with a teasing grin on his face.

"That would be a *yes*!" she snapped.

He jumped off the back of the truck and sauntered over to her.

"Well, I'm mighty sorry about that." The cowboy pulled off his leather glove with his teeth so he could stick out his hand. "I'm Wyatt."

"Casey."

"I do apologize for scarin' you. I hope you can find it in your heart to forgive me."

She took in his dimples, the strong jawline, the masculine chin and the nice teeth to top off his lopsided, flirtatious grin.

Brushing off the flirtation, she said sardonically, "Consider yourself forgiven."

Something akin to surprise mixed with respect flashed in his light blue eyes. "Where did you come from?"

"Chicago." Casey shifted her body away from him, silently signaling that she was planning to end their small talk.

She took a small step back and Wyatt, she noticed, took a small step forward.

"Well, nice to meet you, Wyatt." She gave him a quick wave of the hand.

"It's always a pleasure to make the acquaintance of such a pretty lady." He tipped his hat to her.

His blatant attempt to flatter her, which was obviously a strategy that had worked extremely well for him in the past, made her laugh. It made her glance over her shoulder at him.

What a flirt!

Wyatt was still standing where she left him, grinning at her with both dimples showing. "Hey! Are you kin to the Brands?"

"Niece." She threw this response over her shoulder without looking back this time.

That cowboy didn't need a bit of encouragement. He was way too cute and way too aware that he was cute *not* to be playing the field. A cowboy like Wyatt could probably pick women up just as easily as picking up a gallon of milk at a convenience store.

"Hope to see you around!"

"Goodbye, Wyatt!" She gave another wave of her hand, but resisted the urge to turn around. He was a nice piece of eye candy—that was an undeniable fact. But she had been around the block enough times to know that eye candy like Wyatt was best left on the shelf.

She was, however, still smiling at his flirtation as she hiked up the hill where the chapel had been relocated. At the top of the hill, she paused to catch her breath. The change in altitude made the air thinner; it would take some acclimating before she could hike in the mountains, which was something she genuinely looked forward to doing.

Standing upright, hands on her hips, her cheeks feeling flushed from the exertion and fresh air, Casey stopped to admire the century-old chapel. It had a fresh coat of bright white paint and the curved, wooden door, hand-carved by her ancestor, had been restored.

"Beautiful," Casey said aloud.

After she had caught her breath, she kept on walking. Just over the crest of the hill, Casey spotted the tree that had been planted in memory of Penelope's twin brother, Michael, who had died at birth. She stopped by the oak tree to read the bronze plaque placed in front of the sapling.

Bowing her head, Casey said a silent prayer to her nephew. Tears of sorrow for her sister's loss, and for the loss of the entire family, started to flow without warning. She had thought that she had already cried all of her tears for Michael.

Casey wiped her tears away. Taylor, who had really been more of a mother than an older sister to her, had always taught her to keep moving forward. So, that's what she did. She said a final prayer for her nephew's soul and then walked the short distance to the chapel.

Of course, she wanted to see the inside. But she was saving it for last. She walked all around the perimeter of the chapel, touching the stained-glass windows original to the structure. The chapel, no bigger than a modern one-car garage, was so romantic, set high up on a hill overlooking Bent Tree Ranch, with regal mountains off in the distance. It was the perfect spot for a small, intimate wedding.

"I didn't know anybody else was up here."

For the second time in a relatively short window of time, she had been startled. She had a terrible startle reflex, so even the slightest surprise set her heart racing, made her jump and, when she realized that there wasn't any danger, it made her ticked off.

"Don't sneak up on me like that, Brock! Geez!"

The front of Brock's shirt was sweaty from working, and there was a ring of dirt in the creases of his neck. He was carrying a small cooler in his hand that she had seen him pack with snacks and food for lunch.

"I wasn't really sneaking…" he said. "But I am sorry I caught you off guard."

Her heart was *still* racing. It was a terrible feeling

to have her body overreact over the slightest thing. Having anxiety stunk.

"It's not you—it's me." Casey sighed with irritation. "Lunchtime?"

"I come up here sometimes. I like the quiet."

They both starting walking toward the front of the chapel—Brock had to deliberately shorten his stride to keep pace with her. It seemed to her that if he were walking normally, she would have to take nearly two steps to match his one.

"Have you seen the inside yet?" Brock asked her.

"I was just about to."

At the base of the steps leading to the front door, they paused together. Brock pointed to Michael's tree.

"I like to sit right over there." He pointed to Michael's sapling. "I wouldn't mind the company."

She went up the two small steps to the thick, curved door and Brock headed over to his favorite lunchtime getaway spot. Casey was glad that he didn't join her in the chapel—for a reason she couldn't exactly pinpoint, she had wanted to be alone when she saw it as an adult for the first time.

Walking into the chapel again was like taking a step back in time. She was eight or nine, and this was an enchanted cottage in the woods. Her imagination had taken her so many places when she had played in the chapel as a child—she had been a princess in a hobbit house or a forest fairy with magical gnomes and wild animals as friends. She'd never played "wedding"—it was never that for her.

The renovation had transformed the space from a dilapidated building decades past its glory days to a beautifully preserved representation of turn-of-the-century construction. She had watched the renovation unfold via social media, and she knew that her aunt and uncle had taken every measure to save as much of the original structure as possible. This wasn't the chapel of her memories. This was the chapel returned to its former glory.

"Holy cannoli…" Casey walked along the middle aisle, her eyes flitting from one spot to the next. She wanted to take it in all at once—she wanted to take it in one small piece at a time.

The prayer altar had been preserved and it was there that she found her name carved, by her own hand, into the age-darkened wood. She ran her finger along the groove of each letter and wished she could remember the details of the day when this was carved. She knew that she had been the one to carve it, and it had been carved with her cousin Tyler's pocketknife, but she couldn't recall much more than that. This beautiful, special place was part of her and she was part of it. No matter where she was living in the world, there would always be a piece of Casey Brand carved into the history of Bent Tree Ranch.

Chapter Six

Once she had taken in her fill of the interior of the little building, Casey walked back out into the sunlight. This wouldn't be the last time she visited this place. There was something very special about it—it was intangible, yet palpable.

Brock was propped up on one arm, lying in the grass with his long legs stretched out and his ankles crossed. He had earbuds in his ears and his hat off. When he spotted her, he stood up and waved her over.

"It's unreal in there," Casey said to the ranch foreman. "I could imagine what it must have been like to attend service there a hundred years ago."

"I saved you a spot." Brock gestured to a shady spot next to him.

She hadn't really thought of sticking around. In fact, she wanted to get back to the barn and start working with Gigi.

"I've got water and plenty of food to share." Brock opened the top of his cooler. "Are you hungry?"

Actually, she was a bit hungry. Her aunt didn't know she was a vegetarian, so she had only had salad and corn bread. The hike up the hill in the fresh air and sun had made her stomach start growling.

He must have anticipated that she was being persuaded to stay, because Brock seemed to her like he was trying to close a deal.

"I have egg salad made from eggs produced by free-range chickens."

Casey laughed. "Okay—you know you had me at free-range…"

She sat down in the shady spot, cross-legged. Brock tilted his hat back on his head and sat down next to her. He handed her a bottle of water after he had wiped the condensation off.

"Thank you."

He dug around in the cooler and pulled out a piece of fruit. "Peach?"

She loved peaches. "Thank you again."

Brock also offered her one of his two sandwiches, but she was happy with her peach. She bit into it and juices from the peach dripped down her chin.

"Mmm. This peach is incredible!"

He glanced at her while he was taking a large bite of his sandwich. "Here…" He reached into his cooler and pulled out a couple of paper towels.

She smiled at him and wiped off her chin. Casey didn't try to make conversation until she had eaten the peach all the way down to the center seed.

"That was a delicious peach."

"Good."

That was all that was said between them for a while—they enjoyed the breeze and the sunshine and the quiet together.

"What were you listening to?"

Brock cleaned off his hands, tossed his trash into the cooler, then held out one of his earbuds for her to put up to her ear. She listened, her brain sorting through her memories to put a name with the sound.

After a second or two, she looked up at him, surprised. "Beethoven?"

"Bach."

In the short time she had spent with him, this man had already surprised her a couple of times. He was burly and masculine and the antithesis of a metrosexual, and yet, he seemed to have...*depth.*

"I'll show you the best way to enjoy it," he told her. "Lie on your back."

If it had been anyone *but* Brock, she would have thought this was a ploy to get her in a compromising position—but Brock was straightforward. If he wanted her in a compromising position, most likely he'd come right out and say it.

She lay flat on her back in the grass, both earbuds in her ears.

"Now, close your eyes and let the music take you on a ride," Brock said with an enthusiastic smile. She could tell that he felt as if he was sharing a very exciting secret with her.

"I'm not a big fan of classical music," she warned him.

"Don't focus on that," he instructed. "Just close your eyes, try to turn off your thoughts and listen."

Casey's eyebrows rose as she gave a little shrug and then closed her eyes. Eyes closed, cool breeze brushing

over her arms and face, and the music in her ears—
it was…

She opened her eyes and saw Brock watching her
expectantly.

"Well?"

She pulled the earbuds out of her ears and handed
them back to him. "I liked it."

Brock pulled the cord out of his phone. "There's no
reason why we can't both enjoy it."

It wasn't her nature to take afternoon naps and she
usually ate lunch on the go at work. But she needed to
force herself to slow down. She was on her first true
vacation in years, after all. So, side by side in the grass,
not close enough to touch, but close enough to enjoy
the lilting strains of music, Brock and Casey spent
the rest of the foreman's lunch break quietly together.

By the end of her first month in Montana, Casey
had settled into life on Brock's ranch as if she had
been born to it. She had put her own homey touches
on the loft and now it felt like her own cozy cocoon.
Of course, during the heat of the day, some of the less
pleasant smells from the barn did waft upward and it
could be rather pungent. But it wasn't anything that
an open window couldn't fix. Casey had struck a deal
with Brock to rotate the cooking and pay a fourth of the
food cost, in light of the fact that Brock ate enough to
be counted as two people. The loft didn't have Wi-Fi,
so whenever she needed to use the internet, she took
her computer to the main house. Brock always left the
front door open for her, which allowed her to come and
go as she pleased. The idea of an unlocked door, coming from Chicago, took some getting used to.

Hannah had slowly adjusted to her new routine—during the week she attended summer school and on the weekends she worked with Casey. Casey was able to spend a lot of time with her sister and her niece. She had been working with Gigi regularly, she visited Bent Tree at least once a week and she was still plugged into what she loved to do: work with students with disabilities. At night, after dinner, and after Hannah had gone to bed, Brock and Casey would sit outside on the front porch together. Some nights they talked; some nights they didn't say hardly anything beyond "good night." And on the days she went to Bent Tree, she found herself walking up to the chapel to sit with Brock and listen to the genius of Bach and Beethoven and Tchaikovsky beneath Michael's oak tree. Casey couldn't remember a time in her life when she had been more content or relaxed. As it turned out, Montana was her idea of paradise.

"You coming out to Bent Tree tomorrow?" Brock asked her.

The dishes were done and they were relaxing, as was their way, on the porch.

Casey made a small circle with her finger on the top of Hercules's head. "Uh-huh."

"Do you want to meet me at the chapel?" he asked her after a pause.

She looked over at Brock's profile. It was a strong, masculine profile—hawkish, prominent nose, squared-off jaw. He wasn't a classically handsome man, but he was a man's man with some pretty appealing twists—like his dedication to being a father and his love of animals, his protective nature and his work ethic. The fact that he preferred to listen to classical music instead of country made him interesting to Casey. There was a lot to like about Brock; there was a lot there to respect.

"Sure." She nodded with a smile. "I'll pack lunch for us."

"Even better." He gave her a small smile with a quick wink.

She was just about to ask what kind of sandwich he would fancy—he liked ham and Swiss cheese on wheat bread with extra mustard—but the ringing of his cell phone stopped her from asking him the question.

Brock tugged his cell phone out of his front pocket, looked at the name on the screen and his expression changed.

He stood up. "Excuse me."

She gave him a nod to let him know that she had heard him. The screen door slammed behind him as he went inside the house. The nights were cool enough to leave the windows and the front door open for a cross breeze, so even though Casey didn't really want to eavesdrop on Brock's end of the conversation, it was impossible not to do it.

"No. Absolutely not. We already covered this in mediation."

Brock's voice started out fairly calm, but got increasingly agitated and forceful as he verbally volleyed with his soon-to-be ex-wife.

"We already *covered this in mediation*!" he repeated loudly.

At night, on the porch, and when they were in a talkative mood, they covered a wide variety of subjects. But there were two subjects they never broached: Shannon and Clint. They were two very emotionally charged subjects that both felt very comfortable avoiding.

"Shannon," Brock said and waited. *"Shannon,"* he repeated. "Damnit, I'm sick to death of talkin' about this with you," he snapped at his estranged wife. "Listen…listen…*no*…you listen! We'll either work this out in mediation…we'll either work this out in mediation *or* we go to court. Your choice. But I'm not selling the house. This is Hannah's home and I won't let you take it away from her. You've already got her so twisted up in knots with all of this *BS* you pulled, the doctor's had to adjust her meds *twice*."

Brock stopped talking, so Casey assumed that he had ended the conversation without saying goodbye. A minute or two later, the screen door swung open wide and Brock strode out onto the porch. He walked straight ahead to the railing post and rested his hand against it, his head lowered. He shook his head a couple of times before he banged the post with his closed fist.

"You ever been married?" he asked her without turning his head.

"No," Casey answered him quietly. She hadn't meant to know this much of his business; they were becoming friends of a sort, but they weren't confidants.

"I'm surprised." Brock took the rocking chair next to her. "You seem like the settling kind."

She didn't respond. She had always wanted to get married—hoped that she would while she could still have several children. Women were still having children into their forties, with some assistance from modern medicine, so she still had time. But she had considered freezing her eggs, just in case Mr. Perfect didn't show up in the next couple of years.

"I'm the settling kind, too." Brock seemed like he needed to talk.

Casey didn't mind listening.

"I always wanted to be married—have a wife, kids, the white picket fence. My mom took off when I was young. Hell, I wouldn't recognize her if I saw her in a picture. Matilda. Pop used to say her name like he was talking about a saint—she broke his heart. Left him to take care of me. Then Clint's mom broke his heart a second time—he adopted her kid and then she takes off, too. But, this time, good ol' doormat Dave—he didn't recover. He smoked himself right into an early grave. And I got stuck raising Clint who never failed to do the wrong thing."

At least now she knew why Brock hated her sister's husband so much—he blamed Clint and his mother for his father's death.

"I wanted that family I never had growing up. I wanted it *so bad* that I think I pushed it on Shannon." He nodded his head at himself. "I did. I pushed it on her. She never really wanted this life. Truth be told, between you, me and that fence post…" His voice lowered so that his next words would only reach her ears. "She never wanted to have kids."

Casey had been staring straight ahead at the darkening horizon. When Brock confessed to her that Hannah's mom might not have wanted her, she couldn't stop herself from sucking in her breath and turning her head to look at the man beside her. She understood why many women didn't want to have children. That was what they wanted out of life and that was okay. But to know this about Shannon and Hannah, it made her feel sad for all of them.

"I'm sorry." It was trite and stupid—yet it was all she could muster.

Brock stopped rocking and leaned forward so his elbows were resting on his thighs and his head was in his hands.

"All of this—all of this fighting about custody and about selling the house—that's not really what all of this is about." He sat back up. "Months of mediation, and the plain truth is that she's not going to stop until she gets what she wants."

"What does she want?"

"Taj." Brock gave a small shake of his head. "She wants Taj."

"Hey! Can I interest you in a ham and Swiss on rye?"

Casey appeared at the top of the hill, her face flushed from the wind and the climb up the hill to the chapel. She was smiling that smile that he had grown very fond of over the last several weeks. That smile transformed her girlish, impish, unremarkable face into something quite lovely. It had not escaped his notice that he had been staring at the top of that hill for fifteen minutes waiting for his tenant. It also had not escaped his notice that he felt a sense of excitement and anticipation on the days he knew Casey was going to meet him at the chapel for lunch. He would think about her arrival all morning—and much to the amazement of his men, he would let everyone finish a couple of minutes early for lunch.

He was genuinely happy to see her. That's what he was feeling—happiness. Perhaps it felt odd because it had been a long time since he had actually *felt happy*.

"Do you want to spread this out for us?" Casey held out the blanket she had brought with her.

Brock shook out the blanket and then laid it down

in the spot that had become their favorite place to eat lunch together.

"What's on the menu for you?" Brock held out his hand to help her sit down.

Casey was a petite woman; her hand felt dainty and fragile in his oversize hand. But he knew Casey wasn't fragile—she was a tough cookie. And she was a lot tougher than she looked by a long shot.

"Avocado and Swiss on rye." She sat cross-legged on the blanket.

Casey reached into her basket, a basket she'd borrowed from her aunt, and pulled out two fat sandwiches for Brock and a bottle of water.

"Didn't Hercules make the trip?" He unwrapped a sandwich and took a giant bite. "Mmm. So good. Thank you."

"Hercules is with Aunt Barb—she's obsessed with him. And, of course, he's not going to say no to all of the attention."

They chatted easily while they both ate their lunch. Brock thought that Casey looked particularly nice today—she had opted to wear her superthick, waist-length red hair loose today. Usually she wore it in a ponytail or a single braid down her back—not today. Today it swirled around her shoulders, wispy strands dancing on the wind, as shiny as Christmas tinsel in the afternoon sunlight. He wanted to reach out and see how soft it was to the touch. It looked soft.

"I'm going to have to cut lunch short today, I'm afraid." Casey balled up her wrapper and tossed it into the basket. "My sister is having an 'I'm almost forty' crisis."

He was disappointed—he had a new concerto he

wanted to share with her. And there was something he wanted to talk to her about—something that he knew needed to be said.

"What kind of crisis?"

"She needs glasses." Casey laughed. "I told her I would go pick out glasses with her. She's all worried because she thinks glasses are going to make her look old, and here she is a cougar—married to a younger man."

The words came out of her mouth and she wished she could reel them right back in. It was hard to constantly avoid talking about Clint when he was such a huge part of Taylor's life. And, while she knew Brock had his reasons, however unreasonable, she genuinely liked Clint. He loved Taylor and he was a good father to her niece. Whoever Brock was remembering his stepbrother to be wasn't there anymore. Clint had changed. It surprised her that Brock, who was known to be a tough but fair man, hadn't been willing to forgive Clint for his past transgressions.

After an uncomfortable silence, Brock cleared his throat several times. She looked at him curiously.

"Are you okay? Do you need another water?"

He shook his head.

"No. I'm just trying to get some words unstuck." Brock looked over her shoulder before he brought his eyes back to hers.

"I shouldn't have said all that stuff about Shannon last night," he finally said to her. "I don't want you to think she's a bad person. Because she's not."

Her eyes widened a bit at the turn their conversation had just taken. She had hoped that it was a moment that would just slip away, forgotten by the both of them.

"I don't want you to think that she's a bad mother," he continued.

"I don't." She furrowed her brow.

"She loves Hannah."

"I'm sure she does." Casey leaned back from him a bit and crossed her arms in front of her body.

"She'll always be Hannah's mother," he added as if he was saying it to himself instead of saying it to her.

He stopped talking then, and it took her a couple of minutes to figure out what she should say to him.

"We all need to vent sometimes, Brock." She uncrossed her arms to briefly touch his hand. "All it means is that you're human. I was there to be a sounding board—and I promise you, I'm not a reflective material. What you said won't be repeated."

Chapter Seven

"What do you think of these?" Taylor was modeling a pair of Vogue eyeglass frames.

Casey was in charge of pushing Penny's stroller, carrying Hercules on her arm and providing honest feedback for eyeglass frames.

She wrinkled her nose a bit and shook her head. "Uh-uh."

"Really?" Taylor looked at her reflection in the little mirror on the eyeglass display. "I thought they made me look sophisticated."

"Uh-uh," Casey repeated.

Taylor took off the frames and put them back on the display. "I've tried on almost all of the ones I like. I have to find something—turns out I'm blind as a flippin' bat!"

"What about these?" Casey handed her sister a pair of rimless frames.

"And the doctor tells me that I'm right on schedule—that when most people hit forty, their lens hardens and becomes less flexible. As if that really helps! Any way you slice it, I'm getting old." Taylor tilted her head and studied her reflection. "These aren't so bad. What do you think?"

Casey took a nice long look at her sister before she nodded and said, "Those are the ones."

Taylor got fitted for her glasses and then they decided to stop for a bite to get a caffeine infusion before Casey headed back to Brock's ranch. Taylor moved her straw around in her iced coffee, took several sips and then said, "When I talked to Aunt Barb yesterday, she said that you borrowed one of her picnic baskets to have a picnic with Brock?"

Casey knew that information traveled quickly in the family, and she hadn't told Aunt Barb *not* to mention the picnic basket. Why would she? She wasn't doing anything wrong, after all.

Taylor continued, "I guess I was just surprised that you would be spending so much time with someone you know has been a really negative person in my life. It's one thing to stay on his ranch and work with his daughter—but a picnic?" Her sister shook her head with a frown. "I just don't know why you would do that."

Casey was holding her niece, making her smile and laugh by playing peekaboo. "Tay—I'm trying to stay out of the middle of the family feud. I know that Clint and Brock have a problem with each other, but why does that mean that I can't have him as a friend? He's been really good to me, actually. And, as my sister, I would think that that would mean something to you."

She could tell that her words had struck a chord with her sister, but not enough to swing her opinion about Brock. Taylor shook her head and looked away, her brow furrowed. "I don't even understand what you would have in common with him. He's so...stuffy."

"He's not stuffy," Casey blurted out too quickly not to be noticed by her sister's keen ears.

"Huh..." Her sister put her drink down on the table harder than necessary. "That sounded awfully defensive."

"I'm not being defensive," Casey said in a sing-songy voice while smiling at her sweet niece. "Am I, Penelope? No, I'm not..."

"Is there something going on between the two of you?"

Casey held up her niece and smelled her. "Wooo! Penny! You stink. Here, Momma. This little piggy needs to go home and get changed."

Taylor took her daughter. "Nice try. What gives?"

They both stood up and prepared to drive the short distance to Taylor's rental house. Taylor could be a bit of a germophobe and wasn't crazy about changing Penny in public bathrooms and usually avoided it if she could.

"Nothing," Casey said—and when her sister gave her a look that said *I don't believe you*, she added, "I'm serious. He's going through a divorce and you know I don't do drama."

"But you like him, Casey." Taylor seemed genuinely puzzled by this fact. "I can tell."

Casey got into the passenger seat of Taylor's green Avalanche. "Well, yeah—I do. He's fun to be around."

"Not possible."

"Everyone experiences people differently." Casey shrugged a shoulder, not really wanting to talk about Brock. Perhaps it was because Taylor's questions were hitting a bit too close to home. She did enjoy spending time with Brock. He was nice and kind and liked to eat good food and listen to classical music on his lunch break. He was interesting.

Yes. She did like Brock McAllister. A lot.

"People aren't always what they seem," Casey said thoughtfully. "He's…introspective. He loves classical music."

"You hate classical music," Taylor reminded her. "You used to throw a fit every time Mom and Dad took us to the symphony."

That was true. She did used to hate classical music. But the way Brock introduced it to her, explaining the intricacies of the arrangements and the reason each instrument mattered to the composition of the piece, made classical music interesting through his eyes. And something that used to irritate her and make her feel impatient actually made her want to lie back, close her eyes and let the melody take her on an adventure.

"All I know is that Brock treats my husband like a second-class citizen. And my loyalty is to Clint. If Brock doesn't like the father of my child, then it's going to be really hard for me to overlook that."

Taylor should be loyal to her husband. But did that mean that Casey had to be loyal to her sister and stop spending time with Brock? Was the fact that she liked Brock a betrayal to her sister?

"I feel like you're expecting me to dislike someone just because he doesn't get along with Clint. That's not right, Tay."

Her sister pulled into her driveway, shifted into Park and turned off the engine. Hands still on the steering wheel, Taylor turned her body toward her.

"Maybe it is wrong, Casey. But I don't want you to end up with someone who I wouldn't invite to my house for the holidays."

Casey laughed with a shake of her head, breaking the tension. "Lord have mercy, Taylor! You have me married off to Brock and all I've done is have a picnic with the man! Let's not get ahead of ourselves."

Taylor stared at her—her eyes very intent on her face. "You don't see it, but every time you talk about that man, you smile like it's Christmas morning."

Every day, weather permitting, Casey went for a ride. To be riding again, especially such a beautiful palomino mare like Gigi, was beyond any of her original hopes for her summer vacation in Montana. To be given a horse for the summer—well, it was the greatest gift Brock could have given her and he had done it without having the faintest clue how much it would mean to her.

It was the day after her visit with her sister and she couldn't seem to get the conversation out of her mind. She was hoping that a long ride on Gigi would clear her head.

It was obvious why this was still bothering her— Taylor had a front-row seat to her developing affection for Brock. Just what were her feelings for Brock and was she getting too close to the rancher? It would be one thing if he were single and emotionally stable— but he wasn't single and the impending divorce from Shannon, understandably, had him shaken.

And yet, she couldn't stop herself from liking him. He was a tall, burly man who liked to cook and was a good father. He wasn't her physical type necessarily, as she often gravitated to more metrosexual kinds of guys—and Brock was the polar opposite of that. But that was just the outside. On the inside, Brock was exactly her cup of tea.

Casey swung the saddle onto Gigi's back after she groomed the quarter horse and picked out her hooves. After Gigi was saddled and bridled, Casey led her through the gate and then closed it behind them. She mounted and walked Gigi toward the open field, leaving the reins long so the horse could stretch her neck down while her muscles warmed.

Once Gigi's muscles were nice and loose from the heat of the sun and the walking, Casey clucked her tongue a couple of times to signal to the mare that she wanted her to start into a nice, easy jog.

"Good girl, Gigi!" Casey sunk down into the saddle to stabilize her seat. "Nice jog!"

Casey took Gigi through her paces, working her out at each gait, until Gigi was allowed to do what the mare loved to do: gallop. Casey stood in her stirrups, taking weight off the saddle, gave the mare her head and pressed the mare's barrel belly with her calves. Gigi jerked forward into a gallop, her legs churning, her hooves pounding on the hard earth. They galloped across a wide-open field, kicking up clumps of dirt and sending birds, who had been grounded in the bush, flying into the seemingly endless blue of the cloudless sky.

Paradise. I'm in paradise.

At first, when she heard a pounding noise nearby,

she thought it was the sound of her heartbeat thumping in her ears. But the louder the pounding got, the more she realized that the pounding was coming from behind her. She looked back quickly and saw Brock galloping toward her on Taj. The powerful Taj was twice as fast as Gigi, so it wasn't hard for Brock to catch her.

"Hey!" She smiled at him when they were side by side. "What are you doing?"

"I thought I'd join you for a ride."

They both slowed their horses to an animated walk. Gigi threw her head and nipped at Taj when he got too close to her.

"Man—does she look good. She's lost weight. Her muscle tone is rock solid."

Casey patted the palomino's neck. "She's such a great horse. I can't thank you enough for letting me have her for the summer."

Brock smiled at her. "Like I said—you're doing me a favor."

"Some favor." Casey laughed.

They rode together until they reached the end of Brock's land. Her face felt windburned, her thighs hurt from riding every day and she had more freckles on her face than she had had since she was a kid. But she really couldn't care less. This was an exhilarating way to live—and even though she genuinely missed going downtown to Water Tower Place with her friends and shopping the eight-level mall of fabulousness, it wouldn't hurt her feelings to ride like this every day of her life. Even if she did divert some of her shopping budget to renting a horse or buying a horse and stabling it on the outskirts of the city, there was no way she'd ever have the freedom to gallop across a flat, open field until the horse was dripping with sweat. The best she would be able to do was ride in an arena—it just wasn't the same.

They headed back to the barn—Brock needed to cool Taj down, rinse him off and then get on the road to pick up Hannah from school. The easy silence between them carried them back to the gate. Brock leaned down, unlatched the gate and pushed it open for Casey to ride through first.

"You should take Gigi to one of the local shows—put her through her paces. The two of you have an unusual look that would grab the attention of the judges."

Casey halted the horse and swung out of the saddle. She loosened the girth before bringing the reins over Gigi's head.

"I don't think so."

"Why not?"

Why not?

Performance anxiety. Abject fear.

"It's not really my thing." She shrugged off the suggestion.

"Well, let me know if you change your mind—I could get a friend of mine to hook you up with some Western pleasure show clothes."

"Mmm. Nah." Casey wrinkled up her face at the thought. "Not even for new pretty clothes."

Brock pulled his saddle off the Friesian; Casey knew two things for sure about Brock—he loved Hannah and he loved Taj. Every morning before the sun came up, Brock was in the barn grooming Taj. Almost every night, Brock was riding Taj—keeping him limber and fit. After the night Brock had confided in her that Shannon wanted Taj, she had never questioned him further about it, but that didn't mean she hadn't thought about it. Of course, she could understand why Shannon would want the stallion. He was beyond magnificent. But he belonged to Brock—he belonged *with* Brock. Ever since he had told her about it, she had silently prayed that he won that battle with Shannon.

She took care of Gigi, went to go get Hercules from the loft and then, since it was her night to cook, she headed to the kitchen while Brock headed out to get Hannah. She was going to make gluten-free lasagna—one vegetarian pan and one with Italian sweet sausage because it was Brock's favorite—but it had a long prep time so she needed to get started right away. The kitchen as usual was a disorganized mess. The dishes were all washed, but were piled in the dish drain and on the counters—everywhere but where they should be. Her desire to have everything in its place made it very difficult to work in the kitchen. She had been sucking it up because she was a guest on Brock's ranch. But she'd been around long enough to begin to make some changes to the inside of the house. And she had the autism research on her side—this chaos was not helping Hannah's anxiety or behavior. Hannah needed order and structure and a clean, organized environment. She wasn't just trying to meddle for no good reason. She was meddling for a *very good* reason.

"I've got to get a handle on this." Casey stood with her hands on her hips, feeling overwhelmed by the stacks of dishes and pots and silverware scattered about.

In fact, when she looked beyond the kitchen to the living room, everything in the house felt congested. The flow was bad. The colors were bad.

"Brock and Hannah need feng shui in their lives," Casey decided aloud. "This whole house needs to be rearranged, reworked and decongested."

It was decided. Now all she had to do was get Brock on board and figure out how to completely unclutter and unclog the dilapidated farmhouse without sending Hannah into a tailspin.

Later on, over piping hot plates of gluten-free lasagna, Casey broached the subject of changing the interior of the house. It made sense that the work she had already been doing with Hannah would continue, but it would continue within the context of having the preteen take control of her own environment. Instead of her feeling that the changes were happening to her, she would be the one in charge of the change. Brock surprised her by being open to the idea.

"What do you think, Hannah? Are you up for a little renovation?"

Hannah was eating her second helping of the vegetarian lasagna. "I hate the carpet."

Casey couldn't disagree with her—the carpet was a hideous throwback from the seventies. It gave her the heebie-jeebies just thinking about what might be living in that gnarly shag.

"It's definitely got to go," Casey agreed.

"Well." Brock dropped his napkin on his plate. "Make a list and we'll get started."

That was all the encouragement Casey needed. At home, her apartment was basically the size of the kitchen. It was tiny and she had already feng shui'd it, rehabbed it and decorated it several times over.

Now she had an entire house with which to go crazy?
Heaven.

Hannah and Casey spent the next hour writing a priority list for the house while Brock watched TV. They both agreed that the living room was the first room to be tackled. Even though Hannah wanted to be there for every inch of the demolition fun, they decided that it would be better if Casey got started first thing in the morning before Brock had a chance to think about it and change his mind.

So, first thing after breakfast, right after Brock and Hannah left for school, Casey did what she had wanted to do since the very first moment she had walked into the dreary living room—she began to pull down the awful brocade curtains that must have been hanging there since the house was first built. One by one, the curtains were yanked down, leaving plumes of dust hanging in the air and flying up Casey's nose.

"Achoo!" Casey started to sneeze. *"Achoo!"* She sneezed again and again until her eyes were watering and her nose was running.

She left the pile of curtains in a heap in the center of the living room and ran to the bathroom.

"Oh, lord." Casey looked at her reflection. Her eyes were swollen from the dust; the end of her nose was red from her itching it. She splashed water on her face, hoping to get the dust out of her eyes and her nose. It was in her hair, on her shirt, *inside* her shirt, on her pants—the fine dust that had accumulated for years had landed on her.

She came out of the bathroom only to hear the faint noise of a micro-poodle sneezing.

"Oh, not you, too, Hercules!"

The teacup poodle had been sleeping contentedly in his carrier—but he wasn't sleeping now. She had thought that she had put him out of range and out of danger from the dust, but she had miscalculated the sheer quantity that had been collected on Brock's curtains.

Hercules sneezed once, twice and then again and again, until she lost count.

"I'm so sorry, sweet boy!" Urgently, she got the poodle out of the house and up to the loft where she kept a bottle of liquid Benadryl to control Hercules's allergies.

She was just finishing tending to her micro-poodle and he had just stopped sneezing, thankfully, when she heard a truck pull up. Assuming it was Brock returning to the ranch because he had forgotten something, she hurriedly went downstairs to meet him. But when she reached the bottom of the stairs, she saw that the truck stopping in front of the house didn't belong to Brock at all.

"Howdy!" Wyatt, the flirtatious cowboy from Bent Tree, hopped out of his early model Ford truck.

"Hi."

Wyatt met her halfway. "I took a chance that you'd still be here."

Taken aback, Casey's eyebrows lifted and then drew together. "You're looking for me?"

Wyatt adjusted his brown cowboy hat on his head. "I'm looking for you."

"Why?"

The stark confusion in her single-word question made the young cowboy laugh. Man, oh, man was Wyatt easy on the eyes. So handsome—golden skin, dark gold hair, good nose, straight teeth, deadly dimples… Wyatt must have been leaving broken hearts and broken dreams all over the state of Montana. He wasn't of a settling age, but she had no doubt that female after pining female had given it their best shot to wrangle him.

"I've been trying to catch you at Bent Tree, but I keep missing you. I was starting to wonder if you were avoiding me." Wyatt smiled at her. "But then I thought—that's not possible."

Now it was Casey's turn to laugh. It was a foreign concept to Wyatt that a female wouldn't be swooning at the thought of his baby blues—she didn't have the heart to tell him that she had forgotten about their brief meeting in the barn.

Wyatt reached out and pulled some chunks of dust out of her hair. "You look like you've been rolling around in a dustbin."

"Close." Casey laughed. "I was trying to get rid of Brock's curtains. I'm afraid I lost that battle."

"Do you need a hand?"

She actually did need a hand. But it struck her as weird that the cowboy had stopped by to see her in the first place.

"No. I've got it." She put her hand up to shield the sun from her eyes. "Why'd you say you were looking for me again?"

Chapter Eight

Wyatt didn't get to answer that question, because Brock pulled up and parked his truck right next to the Ford.

Brock didn't look happy to see Wyatt. The ranch foreman's strides were long and determined, and he covered the distance between them quickly and with purpose.

"I wasn't expecting to see you here, Wyatt."

"I was just stopping by to see Casey." The young cowboy held his ground, which impressed Casey. Brock was a big man with a big presence, *and* he was this cowboy's boss.

Brock looked at his watch. "Last I checked, you're supposed to be saddled up and heading up to the north pasture to move the herd."

Wyatt grinned sheepishly—he winked at Casey. "Busted."

"You're late," Brock snapped.

The cowboy tipped his hat to Casey. "Have a nice day."

Wyatt gave one last wave of his hand before he disappeared down the driveway.

Brock stood watching him for a minute; he turned to her. "What was all that about?"

Casey shrugged. "Beats the heck out of me."

"Huh." Brock's jaw was tense—his lips thinned. "I expected to find you tearing apart my living room."

"I was!" Casey explained. "But I caused poor Hercules to have an allergy attack. I had to give him a shot of Benadryl and left him in the loft so he can get some rest."

"Let's go take a look."

Once inside, they both stared at the lumpy pile of heavy brocade curtains she had left in the middle of his living room. She looked between the curtains and Brock to see a reaction—she was pleased to discover that he wasn't upset.

"Well…" He took his hat off and hung it on one of the hooks in the entryway. "It is much brighter in here. I'll say that."

He rolled up his sleeves and started to haul the curtains outside. The minute he started to move the curtains, the plume of dust was back, and they both wound up coughing and sneezing out on the porch. Somewhere in the middle of coughing and sneezing, Casey started to laugh and so did Brock.

"I think I'm going to need a hazmat suit!"

Still coughing a little, Casey wiped the tears from her eyes. "I can't go back in there. I really can't. I'm allergic to dust."

"You stay out here," Brock said, and she was only too happy to oblige. An allergy attack, once started, could last for days.

Brock covered his nose by tying a bandana around the lower half of his face. He dragged the curtains outside, down the porch steps and away from the house. She let the dust settle a bit and then she braved the inside of the house.

"Seriously," Brock told her when he came back inside, "it's a lot better. What next?"

Casey looked up at him. "Don't you have to go to work today?"

"I can take a day off. I've got time on the books."

Casey looked around the room—the one place her eyes kept landing on was the carpet. "Carpet?"

"I'm game. I've actually been wanting to get rid of this for years—you've motivated me to do it now."

"Well, the question is then—what's going to take its place?"

Brock gave a small shake of his head. "I've always wanted to go with wood."

"You could consider something sustainable—like cork."

He smiled at her with an amused smile. "Let's not get crazy."

Several hours later, Casey was amazed by what they had accomplished. The carpet had been torn out of the living room, the hideous curtains were gone and there was now a nice rug on the living room floor to cover the cold concrete until new flooring could be purchased and installed.

"I'd really like to get rid of the wallpaper—paint the walls with a fresh coat of paint and, of course, paint all of this dark wood white so it's not such a downer in here."

"It'll all get done," he reassured her. "It's started now."

Brock took the rest of the week off from work, and because he never called off from work or took time for himself, Casey's uncle gave him the time without question. Hannah helped them pick out flooring and paint and much of the work got done while she was at school. Casey was relentless when it came to projects—she didn't like to slow down and she didn't like to take a lot of breaks. Brock matched her work ethic and, because of that, by the end of the week the living room had been transformed. Brock removed the wallpaper—a tedious job she was glad to hand over to him. She was in charge of following behind him with a fresh coat of paint. They had picked a pretty light green for the walls that looked soft and inviting, but not too feminine.

"I am beat." Brock slumped down onto the couch.

She had to give the man credit—he didn't give up and he didn't give in. He just kept on working until Humpty Dumpty had been put back together again. Casey joined him on the couch. She didn't have the heart to tell him that the furniture really needed to get taken to the dump with the curtains and the carpet. Baby steps.

"We rock."

Brock put his hands behind his head. "We do rock."

She felt too tired to smile or laugh. She just wanted to melt into the couch and never get up.

"You have paint splattered all over the top of your head," Brock informed her.

Eyes at half-mast, she rolled her head to the side so she could see his profile. "You have paint all over your beard."

"I should probably take a shower," he murmured. "Do I stink?"

"A little ripe—yes." She rubbed her eyes and yawned. "Oh, my stars. So tired."

Those were the last words she remembered mumbling. The two of them fell asleep on the couch, side by side, completely exhausted. And it wasn't until she heard Brock moving around that she realized she was curled up on her side, her face planted in the knotty fabric of the old couch, drool on the corner of her mouth.

Lovely.

"I've got to go pick Hannah up from school." Brock looked worried.

"Okay." Casey pushed herself upright.

"I think we went too far with this thing. She's going to freak out."

"If she does, we'll handle it. We've involved her in the decision-making process, so this isn't going to be a surprise. Why don't you take pictures of it so she can look at them on the way home?"

Brock took pictures of the new and improved, uncluttered and unclogged version of their living room. Even with all of the prepping and priming Hannah to handle the change, it still could be tough going for the first couple of nights. But it had to happen at some point. The house needed to change in order to provide Hannah with the most supportive, stable environment possible. Change was hard—yes—yet Hannah had to learn that it was also a part of life. If Hannah was going to live an independent adult life, Brock had to start developing her coping skills now.

As it turned out, Hannah had several meltdowns over the changes in the house. But when Brock realized that his daughter had to be able to process and cope with change while she still had the benefit of a strong support system, he focused all of his attention on rehabbing the living room. There was still a monumental amount of work to be done in the house beyond this one room, but the living room was the most used room in the house besides the kitchen and Hannah's bedroom, so it was the most important. Casey was impressed with Brock's determination and work ethic—once the man got going, there really wasn't any stopping him. Casey didn't like to take breaks, but Brock was even worse. She constantly had to remind him to hydrate and eat a snack or break for lunch. If the rancher got it in his head that what he was doing was for the betterment of his daughter, he was a man with a righteous purpose. In that way, Brock was very much like her own father.

After a physically taxing week of painting and renovating and cleaning, Casey decided to allow herself the rare luxury of sleeping in and lingering in bed. She had grown attached to her loft—early in the morning, before sunrise, she would hear the horses begin to move in their stalls, whickering as the time when Brock would feed them drew near. Sometimes she would awaken completely and listen to the sound of Brock's deep, distinctive bass voice as he went about his morning routine in the barn. There were some mornings she would meet him in the barn and share the chore of feeding and mucking out the stalls. Occasionally, like today, she would hear Brock's voice and the sound of the horses in a half-asleep, half-awake state. She remembered it happening later, but she had been too tired for the noise to awaken her fully.

"Oh..." Casey felt a cramp in her stomach, so intense that it yanked her out of a dream and slammed her into reality without any warning.

"Oh!" She curled her legs upward and pressed her hands into her stomach. Her body broke out into a cold sweat. She pushed her face into the pillow; tears of pain and confusion were absorbed into the pillowcase.

Hercules started to whine—he licked her cheeks and her forehead.

"It's okay, sweet boy." Casey bit the words out. "Momma's okay."

She pushed herself upright and then immediately buckled forward to rest her head on her knees. She swallowed several times, pushing down the feeling that she was going to be sick.

"Uh!" Casey forced herself to stand up. She pressed her hands tightly into her abdomen as she ran to the bathroom. Hercules was too short to make the jump off the bed—he stood at the edge of it barking in distress.

Casey grabbed the side of the pedestal sink to hold herself up. These couldn't be menstrual cramps, could they? She'd always been irregular and had terrible pain during her periods, but nothing like this. She was bleeding. Hard. As soon as she put a heavy-flow sanitary napkin in place, she fished around in her travel bag for ibuprofen. Still bent over, she fumbled with the top of the bottle until it popped off and fell into the sink. She shook out several pills, the maximum allowed in a day, and stuck her head under the faucet to fill her mouth with water.

She sat back down on the lid of the commode and rocked back and forth, pleading with God to stop the pain. The entire time she was waiting for the meds to kick in, she counted backward and realized that it was about the right time for her to have her period. The last period had been over a month ago on the trip from Chicago to Montana. The cramps had been so bad that time that she'd had to add another day to her travel plan so she could rest in the hotel. Her gynecologist, a woman she went to out of habit and a lack of enthusiasm for going through the hassle of finding a new doctor, diagnosed her with endometriosis and suggested that she get the Depo-Provera birth control shot to control it. When she told the doctor she wanted to think about it and the doctor responded by asking why—Casey knew that the patient-doctor relationship was over for her. She fully intended to find a new gynecologist after her summer in Montana—if her body would just *cooperate* until then!

If she didn't have Hercules to worry about, she would have stayed locked in the bathroom. But the tiny poodle hadn't stopped whining since she had left him abruptly. She would need to get dressed and get him downstairs to go to the bathroom, feed him breakfast and then get right back into bed. At the moment, that little to-do list seemed insurmountable.

Casey slowly pulled on her jeans and her favorite comfy Chicago Cubs sweatshirt. She had just sat down on the bed to push her bare feet into her boots when she heard a knock at the door.

"Casey?"

It was Hannah. Even feeling lousy like she did, she waited to see if the social stories and all of the practice had paid off—would Hannah wait after she knocked? She had been knocking consistently—now for the next step.

"Come in, Hannah."

Hannah bounded in. "I knocked."

"And what else?" Casey prompted in a slightly strained voice. She pasted a weak smile on her face, not wanting to alert the preteen to the fact that she wasn't feeling well.

"I waited."

Casey held up her hand to give Hannah a high five. "Nice work!"

"Do you want me to take Hercules out?"

Blessing from above!

"Yes—thank you." Casey pointed to his bowl and his bag of specialty food for a sensitive stomach. "Could you feed him, too, and then watch him for a bit?"

Hannah was enamored with Hercules and the feeling was absolutely mutual. Brock's daughter couldn't take her up on the offer fast enough.

"Are you coming for breakfast? Dad wants to know."

"Oh, no, honey. Tell him I'm not feeling hungry."

Hannah nodded and then slammed the door behind her. They had made a lot of progress on the entrance, but they were going to have to work on Hannah's exit strategy next.

Casey rolled into the bed with her knees tucked up to her chest, pulled the comforter over her shoulders and closed her eyes. The ibuprofen had begun to take the edge off, but not enough to feel remotely normal. Female problems. What a bum rap. She must have dozed off again because she hadn't heard Brock come up the stairs leading to the loft apartment.

"Casey? It's Brock. Can I come in?"

"Come in."

Brock opened the door to Casey's world. The loft had been transformed with some artfully placed rugs and throw pillows and vases with freshly cut flowers. Admittedly, he hadn't known her all that long, but the one thing he had picked up on was that she liked her breakfast. It didn't matter if it was a light breakfast, like a protein bar, or a heavy breakfast, like eggs made by free-range, vegetarian, happy chickens, Casey ate breakfast.

"I was concerned about you." Brock had his hands tucked into the front pockets of his jeans. "Are you okay?"

What should a woman say to a question like that? Skate around the issue or just be blunt?

"I'm not feeling my best today." She didn't lift her head off the pillow.

Brock pulled a hand-carved wooden chair closer to the bed and sat down. Casey had pale skin, but today it looked pasty and gray. Her cinnamon freckles stood out in stark contrast compared to the paleness of her cheeks.

"What's going on?"

The fact that he had pulled the chair up and sat down signaled to her that he wasn't going to go away without some sort of legitimate explanation.

"Female problems."

He processed the information for a moment, didn't seem fazed, and then leaned forward, his hands clasped.

"Is there something I can do to make you feel better? I think we have a heating pad. Would that help?"

"Thank you. But I think I just want to rest." She tried to smile at him so he was reassured. "I'll feel better by tomorrow."

"I've got to go to work today," he explained, as if he needed to.

"You've been out for a week already," she agreed.

He didn't get up right away. "Are you sure you don't need anything?"

"No—just remind Hannah to bring Hercules back before you leave. Okay?"

Brock stood up and moved the chair back a little. "Will do."

He paused at the door. "You feel better."

"Did Aunt Barb call you about our birthdays?" Taylor raised her voice because Penelope was banging on her brand-new xylophone.

"No." Casey was sitting in the long window seat in front of the large loft window. The cramps had, for the most part, subsided with the help of the ibuprofen. Her bleeding was still unusually heavy, which concerned her, but at least she felt well enough to be out of bed.

"She wants to throw us a birthday party out at the ranch."

Their birthdays were a week apart—she would be turning thirty-five and her sister would be turning forty.

"That would be fun." Casey leaned her head against the window—the cool glass felt nice against her skin.

"I think so, too. I'm just worried about how that would work out with Luke and Sophia…"

"What are you talking about?"

Luke was Aunt Barb and Uncle Hank's oldest boy; he was a retired marine captain and a veteran of the war in Afghanistan. From what she had gathered, Luke had been deployed to Afghanistan five times and had been injured once. Luke was married to Sophia and they had three young children together. Taylor had decided to rent her house in Sophia and Luke's neighborhood so she would have a built-in support system; Taylor and Sophia had become very close friends.

"Oh, I haven't told you. I just found out myself."

"Found out what?"

"Luke moved back to the ranch."

Casey didn't say anything—it took a minute for her sister's words to sink in. "Wait—are they separated? They're not getting a divorce, are they?"

Taylor sighed. "I don't know. Luke has really struggled since he retired—he's been diagnosed with PTSD and it's just taken a toll on their marriage."

"I'm so sorry to hear that." Now she understood what Taylor meant about the birthday party. How would Luke and Sophia feel about being at the party together? Was Aunt Barb, who had a very difficult time not meddling in her children's lives, hoping that the party would be a good reason for them to be back under the same roof together?

Taylor agreed with her. Luke and Sophia were the perfect couple—if they couldn't make it, who could?

"We've got a couple of weeks—let's just see how it pans out. Maybe they'll figure it out by then."

Her sister agreed again and then changed the subject. "You sound tired, sis—usually you've got energy to spare. You okay?"

"Um…" Casey's hand went to her abdomen. "Yeah…

I don't know. I got awakened out of a really sound sleep by horrible menstrual cramps."

"Out of a sound sleep?" Taylor asked, concerned. "That worries me. I mean, you've always had a rough time of it but never that bad. The shots didn't help?"

"Not really," Casey told her. "If anything, I think it's gotten a little worse. The bleeding is really heavy."

Casey recounted her experience with her ex-gynecologist and when she was finished, her sister said, "I think you need to see someone ASAP."

"I'll see." Casey did not want to add a pelvic exam to her list of fun things to do on her summer vacation schedule. No, thank you.

"Aunt Barb has the name of a really good gyno—it's kind of weird that this doctor basically has a monopoly on all of the Brand vaginas in the greater Helena area, but if you can get over that…"

"Say hi to Clint for me. And give that good-lookin' niece of mine a big smooch on the cheek. 'Kay?"

"You got it. Love you."

"Love you."

Chapter Nine

Brock came back to the ranch for lunch. He took Hercules out and then brought Casey some fruit, crackers and cheese to eat. It was a kind gesture—a caring gesture. The man truly had a good heart.

"Hercules wants up." Casey covered her mouth with her hand. She chewed a couple more times and swallowed. "He really likes you."

Brock stared down at the micro-dog at his feet. "I'm still convinced that he runs on batteries."

"Oh, be nice to my baby boy!" she chided the rancher. "He can't help it that he's tiny any more than you can help how big you are."

As if on cue, Hercules yipped and hopped in a small circle.

Brock scooped up the poodle that fit in the palm of his hand—and still had room to spare—with a shake of his head.

"Wait—hold that pose. I want to get a picture of the two of you together. It's like one of those pictures where they put a Great Dane and a Chihuahua together in a shot with a silly caption like 'opposites attract'…"

Casey held up her camera. "You're not smiling."

"I'm not going to…"

"Spoil sport." She took the picture, anyway.

Brock always had a comment about Hercules, but she knew that he secretly liked her canine companion. Instead of putting the poodle on the window seat next to her, or back on the ground, Brock put Hercules on his thigh and went back to drinking his water.

"This was nice of you. You didn't have to…but I appreciate it."

"I'm a nice guy." He gave her a little smile. "I'm glad to see that you look like you feel better."

She raised her eyebrows with a small nod in agreement. She was glad that she looked like she was feeling better, too.

"You know what?"

"Hmm?"

"I've been meaning to ask you about this furniture."

Brock seemed guarded. "What about it?"

"Where'd you get it? It's beautiful. All of the hand carving—the details—it's really well made. I'd love to have a set like this. Did you buy it local?"

Brock finished his water, twisted the top back on and put the bottle down on the floor next to his chair.

"Nope. I made it."

Now it was her turn to look surprised. Casey tilted her head questioningly. She pointed to the bed frame. "You made that?"

"All me."

"No, you didn't." She shook her head. "Really? You made all of this—the dressers, too?"

"Every bit of it." Brock picked at his thumbnail before he chewed on it a bit. "And the rocking chairs."

Casey's mouth dropped open. "Why didn't I know that?"

Brock looked down at the poodle that had made himself at home on his thigh. "I don't know. I suppose I never had a reason to bring it up."

"Well," Casey said, amazed, "you are talented as all get out. I'm telling you that right now. You could sell the heck out of this stuff in Chicago. Are you kidding me? You could sell the heck out of this stuff online— get a website built."

Brock scratched his beard—a beard that had gotten way too long and was pretty salty on the bottom part of his chin. "I don't really tinker with that too much anymore."

"That's nuts. Why not?"

"I don't know. Haven't really thought about it. We had Hannah and it seemed like she took up most of our spare time." Brock handed Hercules over to her.

"Do you want to see some of the stuff I made along the way? Maybe you'd see something you could salvage."

When she hesitated, he added, "It might do you good to get some sun on your face. You're looking a little green around the gills."

"Gee." She rolled her eyes at him. "Thanks a lot."

She grudgingly got up and reached for her shoes.

"Hold Hercules while I put on my shoes, will you? He doesn't want to be on the ground right now. Imagine that everything in your world was giant?"

"Everything in my world looks small." Brock directed his next comment to Hercules. "Especially you."

Brock held the poodle close to his face and the teacup rescue bit him gently on the nose.

"Did you just see that…?" Brock laughed. "He just bit me on the nose!"

Casey stomped her feet into her boots, stood up and flipped her hair over her shoulder. "See? I told you he liked you."

Brock, still carrying Hercules in his hand, took her to a shed set back a ways from the barn. He grabbed ahold of the handle and pulled hard on the sliding door. The door didn't budge, so Brock handed Hercules to her and used both hands to force the door open. Inside of the shed, piled high almost to the ceiling, hand-carved furniture, made with quality wood like oak and maple, had been haphazardly packed. Forgotten treasure.

Casey didn't know what to say. Some of the furniture was showing signs of water damage—the wood was rotting and there was a layer of white powdery mold on the legs of the chairs and on the desktops. The shed was long and wide and filled with all of this incredible furniture that could have been appreciated by someone.

"I don't understand." She looked at him. "Why would you throw all of this incredible furniture in this shed and let it rot?"

He didn't answer her. There had to be more to this story than what he was willing to say. And that was okay.

"You're an artist, Brock," she told him, her eyes trying to distinguish shapes and patterns in the dim light at the back of the shed.

"I know how to use a saw and a hammer. That's all."

"No." She shook her head. "That's not all. You are an artist."

If she weren't starting to feel tired and light-headed, she would crawl on top of that pile and see what was in the back. She'd have to save that activity for another day.

"Were you serious about giving me some of this?"

"You can have it all." Brock waved his hand like the stuff in the shed didn't matter—like it was just a pile of junk. "I'll start pulling some of it out and you can point out what you want."

Casey was blown away by the offer and she had every intention of taking him up on it.

Brock continued after a minute or two of thinking. "I may as well pull all of it out. I can burn what you don't take."

She gasped—literally gasped—at the thought of Brock making a bonfire out of his incredible creations. In fact, that was a fantastic business name—Incredible Creations—handmade in the USA.

"That is not going to happen! I'll take every last chair and table and desk before I let you do that!"

Brock pulled the door to the shed shut with a hard slam.

"You take what you want. If you want it all, I'll be happy to load it on a truck and send it back to Chicago with you."

Her apartment wouldn't be able to accommodate but a couple of pieces, but there wasn't any way she was going to let him burn it like scrap wood. She didn't know what she was going to do with it all—maybe store it until she could find good homes for each piece—but none of it was going to go up in flames. Not on her watch.

They walked side by side in silence. Brock seemed pensive now. This whole thing had to be related to his marriage—and his impending divorce. Nothing else made sense. Why would he give up something that he had obviously loved? Why had he given up something that he was so talented at doing?

"If I asked you to make me something custom, would you consider doing it?"

Brock stopped in his tracks—looked at her.

"No. I'm sorry. I don't do that anymore." He stared at her a minute longer, long enough for her to catch the raw pain in his eyes. "Not for anyone."

The pain and discomfort lasted longer than usual this time, but it did subside. Yet—she couldn't ignore that what she was experiencing simply wasn't the norm. And whatever was wrong—if it was, in fact, endometriosis—it seemed to be getting worse. She didn't like to think it, but she would probably have to go to that doctor Taylor had mentioned. The next time she was at Bent Tree, she'd have to ask Aunt Barb for the name of her doctor and a contact number.

"What's on your agenda?" Brock picked up her plate and took it to the sink for her.

"What?" She had drifted off in her mind. "Oh, gosh. Sorry. I was somewhere else."

He was in the habit of asking her about her plans for the day over breakfast, and then after dinner he would ask her how the day had unfolded. She'd never had any man show this much interest in the mundane details of her life.

"Actually..." she continued. "I was thinking about exploring the shed today. Is that okay?"

"You're feeling up to that?" He stopped rinsing off the plate to look at her.

"I feel much better today." That wasn't exactly true. She was better, but still not 100 percent. But sitting around waiting to feel better made her nuts.

She didn't tell the ranch foreman the entire truth because she had picked up on the fact that Brock, underneath his hard, brick-and-mortar exterior, worried about the people in his life. No sense adding to the burden he was already carrying because of the divorce. A divorce and custody arrangement that seemed to be dragging out and dragging out—it always came down to three things: joint custody of Hannah, selling the house and ownership of Taj. Brock didn't open up much about his ongoing mediation with Shannon—the little he did share with her, away from Hannah's ears, told her they had reached an impasse. Mediation had failed and they were going to court.

Hannah, who had been quietly scrolling through her iPad with her left hand and taking bites of food from her plate with her right hand, asked them, "Did you know that ladybugs are cannibals?"

Casey had been encouraging Brock to redirect some of Hannah's intensive interest in ladybugs to other subjects in order to increase her ability to function more appropriately and socially with her peers. But it was also true that those intense interests or passions that often came with a diagnosis of autism could lead to a career down the road.

"I had no idea," Casey said to her. "I thought lady-bugs were harmless."

"They are harmless." Hannah looked at her so seriously, as if she were defending the honor of a close friend. "They only eat their siblings if food is scarce."

Brock met her eyes and they smiled at each other.

"Well." Casey pushed back her chair. "That's certainly good to know."

The ranch foreman rested his hands on the back of one of the kitchen table chairs—Casey often found herself staring at his hands. They were massive. Not the kind of hands that you would suspect washed dishes or cooked stick-to-your-ribs, down-home country food.

"Come on, Hannah. Get your stuff together. It's time to get you to school."

It took Hannah a little bit longer than other children to shift her focus, but she had made progress.

"Check your schedule," Brock reminded her. "Make sure everything's checked off."

A visual schedule with a list of chores always worked in Casey's classroom, so she suggested that Brock create one for Hannah at home, and it seemed to be reducing the number of outbursts in the morning. Hannah knew what she was expected to do and she was in charge, in control, of getting the chores done and checking them off the list.

Hannah picked up her plate, rinsed it off and put it in the dish drain. Then she checked that chore off her list. Brock waited until he heard Hannah's heavy footsteps reach the top of the stairs before he said, "You've done so much with her in such a short time."

Casey was kneeling down beside the family dog, Lady, who had taken a liking to Hercules—and now the feeling was mutual. They were a very odd pair, but it appeared to be love. Whenever they were in the same room, Hercules would be glued to the yellow Lab, and if Lady was lying down, the poodle would lie down atop her outstretched paws.

Casey didn't want to take credit for Hannah's hard work. All she did was make some changes to the home environment and work on some essential social skills.

"She's a really hard worker." Casey scooped up Hercules. "There isn't any reason why Hannah can't go to college, have a career, get married."

Brock stared at her wordlessly for so long that she was prompted to ask, "What?"

"I'm just not used to hearing someone be so positive about Hannah." Brock's voice had an odd waver in it that made her look closely at his face. "I've heard a lot of negatives for most of her life—what she needs to work on, what her limitations are going to be, behavior plans. I don't hear about all of her strengths much.

"Thank you for that," he added.

Before Brock piled Hannah in the truck, he opened the shed door for Casey. She had promised to be careful; he had warned her to watch out for creepy-crawly inhabitants as well as slithering ones. It was a large shed, the size of a two-car garage but twice as deep. This was going to be a challenge, push her strength to the limit, but she thrived on seemingly insurmountable tasks. It was fun for her and she could happily lose herself in a job like this. She didn't really have a rhyme or reason to her method of how she was going to unload the furniture—she was just going to dig in.

One by one, she untangled loose chairs, easy to

lift and move out of the way. Then she crawled up on top of the pile to reach for the chairs at the peak. It was warming up quickly inside of the metal structure, and several hours into the chore, Casey had to take a break. She had begun to sort the pieces according to style or function. Her favorite pieces were the heavy rocking chairs—Brock could sell these like crazy on a website. She just couldn't understand his stubbornness on the subject.

Casey dusted off one of the rocking chairs, sat down and sighed the sigh of a woman who was feeling a rush of endorphins from exerting her body. She guzzled down a full canteen of water before she closed her eyes and rocked happily in the rocking chair. This chair, for sure, was going back to Chicago with her. She already had the perfect spot picked out for it.

"Howdy!"

Casey's eyes flew open—she shouldn't be hearing anyone else's voice. She was supposed to be alone on the ranch.

Wyatt, the cute cowboy.

"I was beginning to think that I wasn't going to find you." Wyatt walked over her way.

She couldn't help herself—he was young, but boy was he cute. The way his faded blue jeans fit his thighs, the way his hat rested on his head—that smile.

"How are you, Wyatt?" Casey stood up. She supposed her break was over. She'd find out what Wyatt wanted, then send him on his way so she could get back to work. She had it in her head that she was going to pull every stick of furniture out of the shed so she could sort it out. Some of the pieces were damaged beyond repair, but most of the pieces just needed a little love and elbow grease.

Wyatt tilted his hat to her in greeting. "Just another day in paradise."

Her eyes landed on the beautiful mountains in the background, the flat prairie perfect for galloping Gigi and the wide expanse of blue sky. It *was* paradise—or the closest thing to it for her. She had been wondering lately—if she could brave Chicago in the winter, could she survive Montana in the winter?

"Whatcha got going on here?" Wyatt looked at the furniture strewn about.

"I'm unloading this shed," she explained the obvious. "Brock said I'm free to take what I want. It's such beautiful stuff, I wish I could take it all."

"This is Brock's work?"

She nodded. "Speaking of work—aren't you supposed to be at Bent Tree?"

"Day off." He smiled at her.

"And you thought you would just stop by to say hi?"

"Yep." Wyatt took a look inside of the shed. "If you're gonna move all this stuff out of this place, you're gonna need some help."

She tried to decline his help, but he wouldn't hear of it. For some reason, the cute cowboy wanted to stick around. And yes, he was a flirt. But he was harmless. Her aunt and uncle both liked Wyatt—he was young and took wholehearted advantage of his natural good looks, but he wasn't there to hurt her.

"All right—all right." She finally gave in. "If you want to help me, help me. You can start by moving that desk right there."

Wyatt dove into the project and his muscles did

come in handy. Somewhere along the line, he shed his button-down shirt and was bare-chested. He reminded her of the Matthew McConaughey of the nineties, when he took every opportunity to take his shirt off because he knew that he looked that damn good. Well, Wyatt looked that damn good. Golden skin, golden hair, shredded abs, defined arms. He was the whole sexy package.

"Woooo!" Wyatt jumped down from the top of the smaller pile of furniture. "I'm sweating like a whore in church!"

She was trying to woman-handle a heavy desk to its section with only minimal success. She had pulled it, pushed it, cursed at it.

"Wyatt! Would you help me, please?"

The cute cowboy was wiping the beads of sweat from his chest and forehead and face. He tossed his shirt over the back of a nearby chair and then headed her way.

"Here—move on over." Wyatt winked at her. "This is a job for a man."

Oh, really?

"Is that so? Then I suppose I should wait until one arrives, huh?"

Wyatt tugged on the table that was caught on a root in the grass; he laughed at her comment, but kept on tugging until the table was free. The smile of triumph he gave her when he easily dragged the table to its "section" with one arm was so cocky that she couldn't even hold it against him. It was undeniable—Wyatt was flat-out likable.

"Thank you," she said.

The cowboy posed for her like he was in a body-building contest, showing off his biceps. "Count on the guns!"

Casey rolled her eyes. "Yes, yes. I see them." She grabbed his damp shirt and tossed it to him. "Now put them away before you hurt somebody."

Chapter Ten

They worked side by side, only taking breaks for hydration, until the shed was completely empty and every piece of furniture was categorized. The furniture that wasn't salvageable was put off to the side for Brock to handle in his own way.

"Holy cannoli." Casey couldn't believe what they'd accomplished. "That was a chore. Now I've got to figure out how to get it back in there so it's easy to get around."

She walked over to the area of the yard where she had put the several styles of bed frames. There was one in particular that she liked. She moved a couple of things out of her way to get to the bed frame she had in mind to put on the "take to Chicago" list when she spotted something move near her foot.

"Oh, crap! Oh, *crap*!" She scrambled up onto a

nearby desk, stood up and searched the ground for the snake that had just slithered between her legs.

She pointed. "Snake! Right there! Snake!"

Her heart was racing like crazy. She hated snakes. She *hated* snakes. And that one had the audacity to slither right between her boots like he was going under a bridge!

"You're fine." Wyatt brushed off her panic. "It's probably harmless. The only venomous snakes we have in Montana are rattlers. Did you see a rattle?"

She frowned at him. "No."

"Then quit your yelling, woman. He's more scared of you than you are of him."

"*That* is not true!" she snapped at him. "You quit lecturing me and make sure he's gone!"

Wyatt kicked some of the wood around where she had found safe ground. It took a minute, but then she heard him say, "There you are."

"What are you doing? What are you *doing*?"

Wyatt had dived forward, his hand outstretched. When he straightened upright, he had a snake in his hand.

"Look—see? It's just a gopher snake. He's not gonna hurt you." Wyatt started to walk toward her with the snake.

"Don't you dare bring that snake over here, Wyatt! Don't you dare do it!" she hollered. "Take him out to the field—far enough away so he won't come back!"

Wyatt grinned at her, but he didn't come any closer. "He's just a kid. Are you sure you don't want to see him up close so you know another gopher snake when you see one?"

Her heart was beating so hard that it sounded like

a drumbeat in her ears. Her legs were shaking and she felt completely freaked out.

She jabbed her finger toward the field. "Over *there*!"

The cowboy complied with her command—he was laughing good-naturedly on his way to setting the snake free. Wyatt strolled back to where she was still standing atop the desk.

"The coast is clear. Do you wanna come on back down?"

"Which direction did he head?" she asked cautiously.

"He's halfway to Canada by now." Wyatt held up his arms so he could lift her down. "Come on now. I think you owe me a cold drink and some conversation."

Casey let Wyatt swing her down from the desk. Up close, he smelled kind of sweaty and woody and musky, but it wasn't offensive.

"You're just a little thing, aren't you? How tall are you, Casey?" Wyatt asked her as they walked back to the farmhouse to get something cold to drink.

"That's a strange question." Casey lifted an eyebrow at him. "Five two and three quarters. My sister and I totally got gypped in the height department— we took after our mom's side of the family instead of the Brand side.

"Lemonade okay?" Casey asked when she reached the top step of the porch.

"That'd taste mighty good right now."

"Have a seat out here—I'll get it for us."

Casey wasn't sure how Brock would feel about Wyatt being in his house—but if she had to take a guess, it would be that he wouldn't be too fond of the idea.

She reappeared with a pitcher of lemonade and two

glasses full to the rim with ice. She pushed the screen door open with her shoulder and carried the tray carefully over to where Wyatt was kicked back, his boots propped up on the porch railing.

"Here!" He jumped up. "Let me help you with that."

"You're just full of help today, aren't you?"

Wyatt gave her one of his quick winks. "Yes, ma'am."

Did he just ma'am me? Maybe he isn't trying to hit on me.

She poured the lemonade for them, handed him his glass and then sat down. Her body thanked her for sitting down. She was worn-out. And the endorphin high that she had been riding for hours had disappeared, leaving her feeling a pain on the right side of her abdomen again.

"Thank you, Wyatt. Seriously. I was in over my head and didn't know it."

He gulped down the lemonade in one shot and then went back for more. He gulped down a second glass before he came up for air.

"That's darn good lemonade."

She nodded her agreement; when she looked over at the cowboy, she just couldn't stop herself from clearing up any confusion she was feeling.

"Wyatt…I need to clear something up in my own mind. You aren't…hitting on me, are you?"

Wyatt laughed an easy laugh. "I've been tryin'."

Baffled, Casey asked, "Do you even know how old I am?"

He gave her a sheepish look. "I carried your aunt's groceries in the other day. I might've accidentally seen your birthday candles. You're either gonna be thirty-five or fifty-three."

He was trying to make her laugh and it worked. To have such a good-looking cowboy paying attention to her, it was flattering. It really was.

"Just exactly how old are you, Wyatt?" She didn't think that she was all that much older than him in years, but she was light-years older than him in maturity.

"Twenty-four next month."

"I'm a decade older than you." Casey took another sip of her lemonade. "Why do you think you want to go out with me?"

Wyatt looked at her face appreciatively. "I'm a sucker for a redhead."

"And?" she prompted him when he didn't say anything more.

"Does there have to be anything more than that?" Wyatt asked, and for the first time, he actually sounded serious. "I think you're pretty and I want to take you out."

He filled in the empty space in the conversation by adding, "And I personally think you should go out with me. I guarantee that you'd have one of the best nights of your life."

"I'm flattered, Wyatt." She smiled at him. "I really am. But I just think we're the wrong age for each other."

"I'm not asking to get married," Wyatt bantered. "I just want to take you dancin'."

It struck her as out of character that part of her wanted to go out with the cowboy. Yes, he was younger than her, but like he said, he wasn't looking for marriage. He just wanted to take her out for the fun of it.

"I asked your aunt about you." Wyatt stood up and leaned against the railing opposite her chair.

"You asked my aunt about me? How'd that go?"

"She told me that you aren't fast." Wyatt rested his hands on either side of his body. "But I don't mind slow. As a matter of fact, I think I'd like to try out a new gear for a change."

Wyatt helped her repack the shed so that there was an aisle in the middle. All of the furniture was organized now and easy to access. When Brock returned home that evening, he was shocked to see what she had managed to accomplish.

"You did all of this by yourself?"

There was a moment, right before she told him that Wyatt had helped her, that she felt nervous to tell him. No, she hadn't been officially dating Brock, but they had been spending so much time together that it kind of *felt* like something might be building between them. But there was always the divorce hanging overhead like a nasty storm cloud.

"Wyatt was here again?" Brock's heavy dark brows drew together severely. "I need to have a talk with that boy."

"No." Casey wanted to reassure him. "He's not bothering me. Really. He's harmless. And actually, he was a really big help."

"So—did you find anything you wanted?" Brock asked her after he had cleaned his plate.

"Are you kidding?" She was in awe at the man's talent. "Everything!"

"If you've got a place to keep it, you can have it." He was serious, too.

"No—I wouldn't do that. It's too much."

She waited for a moment before she added, "You

are going to get irritated with me for saying this, but you are so incredibly talented, Brock. I just wish you would do something with that gift—it's such a waste if you don't."

"Are you done?" He pointed to her plate; she didn't feel hungry. She would have thought she would be famished—but she wasn't.

He took her plate when she nodded yes in response to his question.

"Why don't you want to make furniture anymore?" She really wanted to know. God-given talent like that shouldn't be squandered for no good reason.

Brock sighed—he had his hands resting on the edge of the kitchen sink, his head bowed down, his back to her.

"I just lost the desire," he finally told her. "I didn't have the heart for it anymore."

His words struck a nerve in her, stirred up a painful memory of love lost from her college years. She used to write poetry—and she was pretty good at it, too—but after her first real boyfriend didn't want to be with her anymore, she lost the desire, the heart, to write poetry, and she hadn't written any poetry since. That was the last time she was going to pressure Brock about it. His heart was broken and she doubted he'd make another stick of furniture until that broken heart was mended.

The family was gathered in the large kitchen of Bent Tree where a long table carved from one of the fallen trees on the property allowed seating for the entire family and guests. It was the room in the house that was always warm, no matter the season, because the ovens were always on. Aunt Barb was an avid cook and loved to make homemade meals and desserts for her family. That was one of the many ways her aunt showed everyone in the family how much she loved them. So, when her aunt insisted on hosting a "semi-surprise" birthday party for her and Taylor, she couldn't refuse. It would hurt her Aunt Barb, and now that she was a regular visitor at Bent Tree, she was feeling less like a stranger and more like family.

Uncle Hank, who had a very nice singing voice, added after everyone else had stopped singing, "And many more!"

Aunt Barb clasped her hands together, her finely structured face lit up with joy because the family had gathered. She was such a family-focused woman—if she could, she would have all four of her living children living on the ranch so she could see them every day and spoil the living dickens out of her grandchildren.

"Make a wish!" everyone shouted at them. The cake had a three and a five on one side for her, and a four and a zero for Taylor on the other side.

"You go first," she said to her sister. Taylor closed her eyes tightly, thought for a moment and then blew out her two candles. Everyone cheered when the candle flames were blown out.

"Your turn," Taylor said. "Wish for something wonderful."

Casey held her long ponytail close to her body so wayward strands wouldn't get caught by the candle flames. She closed her eyes tightly and wished for what she had wished for the last several years: *a family.*

Casey opened her eyes and blew out the flames, first on the number 3 and then on the number 5. The family cheered for her; there was so much love in the room aimed at her, it made her wonder how she would ever go back to her fairly solitary life in Chicago. Yes, she had friends. But most of her friends were married now with children. She was one of the last single friends from college; she didn't blame her friends for not having much free time—if she had the family she wished for, she wouldn't have time to go shopping or go out to eat downtown. She would be at home, with her husband, enjoying her children.

"Thank you, everyone!" Casey blew kisses to her family on the other side of the table. "Let's eat cake!"

Aunt Barb, by her request, had baked a five-layer red velvet cake with thick, rich, buttery, cream cheese frosting. She had her first slice then immediately went back for a second slice.

"Am I too late for the party?" Wyatt came waltzing into the kitchen.

She had already said "no thank you" to the cowboy twice now, but he just kept on coming back for more rejection. At least he rebounded quickly.

Her uncle Hank and her cousin Luke greeted Wyatt without any reservations. They shook his hand and gave him a pat on the back.

"For the birthday girl." Wyatt pulled a single red rose out from behind his back.

Casey's eyes skirted around to her family to see their reaction. This was completely embarrassing. And yet, it was…nice.

She accepted the flower and smelled it right away. "Mmm. Thank you, Wyatt."

"Sit down and have a piece of cake, Wyatt," Barbara said to the new arrival. It was always the more the merrier for her.

Casey was glad to see Sophia and Luke sitting next to each other at the table, each holding one of their twin toddler girls, Annabelle and Abigail. Their son Danny had gone outside to play, and Casey thought that his parents would be glad that he was going to work off some of that rare sugar infusion before bedtime. But even though they were sitting next to each other, there was a weird tension between them. They didn't exchange but a handful of words, and they hadn't touched each other, not even when Sophia had first arrived with the children.

"Do you mind slidin' over a bit?" Wyatt asked Taylor. "I really had my heart set on sittin' next to the birthday girl."

"Woman," Casey corrected. "I'm the birthday *woman*."

Taylor did the unexpected, at least in Casey's opinion—she scooted over to make room for the cowboy.

"She thinks that I'm too young for her." Wyatt grinned at the table full of friendly faces. "How's the collarbone, Clint? I heard you banged it up but good down in Texas."

Clint was sitting next to Taylor, holding a sleeping Penelope in his arms. "It's knitting back together alright."

Taylor didn't say a word, but Casey knew from their conversations that her sister wished her husband's professional bull riding days would soon be behind them.

"You thinkin' about retiring?" Wyatt asked before he put a huge bite of cake in his mouth. He gave Casey a closed-mouth smile while he chewed with a wink.

Incorrigible.

Clint's conflict about his career showed on his face. "It's lookin' that'away."

"So…" Wyatt turned his attention on her. "You've turned me down twice. She's turned me down *twice*," he said louder to the whole table.

"That's a record right there," Luke, who was typically quiet in a crowd, said loudly with a sharp laugh.

"That's got to sting," Uncle Hank said before he took a sip of his coffee.

"That's okay—that's okay—there's more than one way to lasso a calf."

Casey peeked around Wyatt to her sister. "Did he just use a cow metaphor in relation to me?"

"I've decided to ask Ms. Barbara," Wyatt continued loudly, "for her permission to take her lovely niece out dancing to celebrate her birthday."

"That is playing dirty, my friend," Casey said to the cowboy.

"I think it's a wonderful idea, Casey." Aunt Barb beamed at her. "I think you should go."

Brock heard Casey come in from her night out on the town with Wyatt because he had been awake, on the couch, waiting for her to come home. It was inconceivable to him that he had let that smooth-talking cowboy get the better of him with Casey. Not that he had an agreement with the pretty redhead. He didn't. But the minute she'd come home from her birthday party, flushed in the cheeks and telling him in a rush that she had to find something to wear for a night out on the town with Wyatt, he knew that what he had been feeling, and concealing, was more than just a passing fancy. He had real feelings for Casey. He had deep, genuine, impossible-to-shake feelings that he had kept hidden because he was legally married. It didn't matter to him that they were separated; it didn't matter that he knew Shannon had already moved on. It mattered that in the eyes of the law and God, he was a married man.

Oblivious to the anguish he felt at the thought of her getting dolled up for anyone but him, Casey had burst through the screen door to ask him his opinion on her dress. Her beautiful hair had been washed and blow-dried; when she walked, the ends of her hair swished enticingly just above her derriere. He had thought about touching her hair—so many times. She had spun in a circle, in her pretty forest green dress.

"Please be honest…" She looked down at her dress self-consciously. "Does it look like I'm trying too hard?"

"No." He had to tell her the truth. She looked like a genuine cowgirl with that flouncy skirt that ended just above the knees and a new pair of boots. "That dress suits you."

She had hugged him then. It was a spontaneous hug that had nearly bowled him over—he could still feel her arms around his body. They hadn't been that close—not since the first day he had rescued her. He wanted to wrap his arms around her and not let her go. She shouldn't be getting gussied up to go out with any man, unless that man was him.

"You'll watch Hercules, won't you?" she had asked him. "I can't leave him alone up there. He'll be too scared."

Casey had asked him to watch her most beloved thing in the world—Hercules the micro-poodle. So he understood that it meant something that she had en-trusted Hercules into his care. But, and this was a *huge* but—any scenario where he ended up on his couch holding a teacup poodle while Wyatt *damn* Williams got the girl—was a *bad* night.

So, no—he wasn't really asleep when Casey tiptoed into the house at 2:00 a.m., slightly tipsy and humming a popular country tune.

Of course Wyatt tried to kiss Casey. That was the whole point of the pursuit. But the question that had been running around in his mind, over and over, like a skipping record, was: *Did she let him?*

Did Casey let Wyatt kiss her? And, even more important—did she kiss him back?

Casey tried to be very quiet when Wyatt dropped her off, but she was a little wobbly from a couple of celebratory drinks, so she wasn't *as quiet* as she had planned.

In the foyer, she took two steps forward and then two steps back. She spun around, which made her lose her balance.

"Shhhh." She laughed at her near fall into the wall.

On her tiptoes, she went to the couch where Brock always slept, knowing that Hercules would have found a comfortable place to sleep somewhere on that giant expanse of the ranch foreman's body.

"Hi, puppy face!" Casey found Hercules tangled up in Brock's unruly beard.

"Shhhh," she chastised herself. "People are sleeping."

She scooped up her poodle and, after bumping into an end table, she opened the screen door very, very slowly in an attempt to keep the squeaking to a minimum. However, once through the door, she forgot to shut it gently and it slammed back into place, making a loud racket.

"Oh! Shoot!" Casey froze in her tracks. "Darn it! *That* was *not* quiet *at all.*"

Chapter Eleven

On the way back to the loft, Casey hummed and twirled and kissed her poodle on the head happily. What a night! What an incredible, fun, unexpected night! Wyatt hadn't lied—he had shown her one of the best times she'd ever had. He was full of life and he was popular and he was so much fun to hang out with. And the boy could dance. He really could. In fact, he showed her quite a few moves.

They had laughed and talked about nothing important or serious. Wyatt wasn't serious—he didn't follow politics or the economy. He wasn't the kind of guy a woman of her age should allow too far into her life— but for a whopping good time, no strings attached, no commitment required, he was a total blast!

She continued to hum as she opened the door to her loft. Casey put Hercules down and then twirled her way to the bed. She was just about to flop onto the bed when she noticed a present on her bed.

"Ah!" she exclaimed. "A present!"

It was wrapped haphazardly by hands unaccustomed to that sort of activity; there was a giant silver bow on the present and a note card that merely said "Happy Birthday, Casey" in scratchy handwriting.

"What could this be, puppy face?" Casey ripped the wrapping off the present, balled it up and threw it over her shoulder.

In the low light, and looking through wobbly beer-goggle eyes, Casey couldn't immediately tell what she had just unwrapped. But then it hit her—Brock had made something just for her. Something that he knew would touch her heart the most.

"Oh, Brock." Her hand went to her heart. "You dear, sweet, complicated man."

The morning after her birthday, Casey woke up with her first hangover in years. She hadn't "partied" in ages. She was a career woman—she was an educator. Her life didn't involve late nights or drinking more than a couple glasses of wine on the weekend. Last night, in the spirit of letting down her hair and kicking up her heels, she'd had several drinks past her limit. It had been a good time that didn't feel so good the next morning.

When she sat upright in bed, she immediately collapsed forward and dropped her head into her hands. The pounding in her head was so hard—*thump, thump, thump.* Why hadn't she remembered to drink water before she went to sleep?

"Why didn't you just say no to the last three drinks?" she grumbled.

She fell over on her side with a moan. "I'll never do that again."

Hercules barked and that got her attention. She inched over to the side of the bed, pushed her wild locks out of her face and looked down at her canine friend.

"Look at you, puppy paw!" She smiled weakly at the little poodle.

Hercules was the proud owner of a Brock McAllister custom creation. For her birthday, Brock had made Hercules his own miniature bed.

"You like your new bed, don't you?"

If she didn't have Hercules to tend to, perhaps she would have lingered in bed for an hour or two longer— let the headache subside. But Hercules had a thimble-sized bladder, so he couldn't be held accountable for any accidents that were caused by a human being gone longer than his bladder could manage.

"Okay." Casey inched even farther over to the edge. "You can do it."

She slid off the side of the bed and melted downward to the floor. The room started to spin in the most upsetting way. Her stomach started to churn and the next thing she knew, she was on the floor in the bathroom.

"Starting off thirty-five hungover." The cool ceramic of the tub felt nice on her forehead. "Awesome."

First, Hercules got to go out and then he was served breakfast. Then she showered, brushed her teeth for an extended amount of time and then braided her hair to get it out of the way. Her eyes were bloodshot and her coloring looked jaundiced.

"But, besides that—" Casey held up both her thumbs "—two thumbs-up."

She slowly made her way down the stairs and to the kitchen. Brock and Hannah were long gone—it was almost ten. Today was Wednesday—this was the day that she usually met Brock at the chapel. She had a feeling he wouldn't be expecting her, but she just couldn't wait to thank him for the beautiful gift. Her family had been generous this year, spoiling her with gift cards to her favorite shopping haunts and bottles of her favorite perfume. But for Brock to secretly make her a mini version of his incredible bed frames for Hercules? That was another level entirely.

She had a light, bland breakfast, afraid that anything she put in her stomach wouldn't stay there for long. She popped a couple of over-the-counter pain relievers for headaches so she could make the drive to Bent Tree without her head throbbing incessantly. Brock would already have his lunch, and she wasn't up to full speed yet—she opted to not bring anything to eat. She grabbed a couple bottles of water before heading to her loaner VW Bug.

"Come on, puppy face." Casey secured the poodle's carrier with the seat belt. "Let's go see Brock."

Casey dropped Hercules off with Aunt Barb, who was happy to dog-sit for her. She climbed up the hill, the same way and at the same pace as usual. This time, it felt like the hill kept on getting taller and taller and the top kept on getting farther and farther away. She was sweating through her T-shirt by the time she reached the top of the hill.

After making such a physically taxing climb, Casey was disappointed that Brock wasn't in his usual spot. She pulled her phone out of her back pocket and checked the time. It was the right time and the right place. But still no Brock.

"Oh, my head, my head, my head." Casey was flat on her back in the grass, legs stretched out, with her arm over her eyes.

Her cell phone, which Taylor had been blowing up all morning, started to tweet, which let her know that she had just gotten a new text.

With a frustrated noise, Casey texted her sister back:

Yes, I had a good time, no, I didn't let him kiss me, yes, he tried, no, he didn't try to cop a feel and no, neither did I!

Casey turned the volume off on her phone so she couldn't be annoyed by texts or emails, Snapchats or Instagram updates. Her head really needed it to be quiet.

"I was wondering if you were going to make it today."

She lifted her arm from her eyes and stared at an upside-down view of Brock. He looked even taller from this angle.

"I wanted to say thank-you for my birthday present."

Brock sat down in the grass beside her. "I'm glad you liked it. How does Hercules like it?"

"Are you kidding me? He thinks he's King Badass now. He didn't want to sleep with me last night. He slept in his new bed instead."

Casey sat upright; she grabbed her head with a groan. "Headache?"

"Totally my own fault." She tapped the camera icon on her phone to pull up pictures of Hercules in his bed. "Your first satisfied customer."

That got a smile out of him. Was she wrong, or was he extra pensive today?

"I didn't bring anything for you. I really didn't think you'd show."

Casey moved onto her side, resting her head in her hand. "It's fine. Believe me. My stomach isn't happy with me right now. You seem tired today." She noted the dark circles beneath Brock's eyes.

"I didn't sleep so well last night."

"That's because you always sleep on that couch," she said. "You need to sleep in your own bed. If you don't want to sleep on that mattress, then go buy a new one."

The conversation ground to a halt after Brock unpacked his lunch and began to eat. He didn't talk during meals—he focused on the food. But today, she couldn't hold up both ends of the conversation like she normally would. They sat together in comfortable silence; she enjoyed the feeling of the sun on her arms and her face. She closed her eyes and soaked in the vitamin D.

"You had a good time." It was a statement, not a question.

She opened her eyes when she answered, "I did. I can't remember the last time I had that much fun going out. Wyatt taught me the two-step!"

More silence. Brock was in a very strange mood

today. He looked drawn in the face and he had a distant look in his eyes.

"I wish you could have come to my birthday party." She picked at a blade of grass.

She had invited him but knew in advance that he wouldn't come.

"Hannah has never been able to handle parties like that. It's too much stimulation for her."

Casey understood that and she had told him as much. But she also knew that Brock wouldn't have wanted to attend because of Clint. The longer she was in Montana, the more difficult it was to work around that fractured relationship, and honestly, the more annoyed she became with the entire situation.

She had grown to genuinely care for Brock; he was a good man. But when it came to his stepbrother, he really needed to get it together for the sake of the entire family—including Hannah.

Brock stood up abruptly, brushed the loose grass from the seat of his jeans and held out his hand to her.

"I need to talk to you."

"And we need to stand up to do it?" She slipped her hand into his and let him help her stand up.

He nodded toward the chapel. "Let's go sit on the steps."

A shrug. "Okay."

Brock, ever a gentleman, waited for her to be seated comfortably before he sat down beside her. Looking at their bodies side by side, Brock's legs were almost twice as long as hers.

The ranch foreman looked straight ahead with his standard-issue Stetson sitting squarely on his head—

his elbows were resting on his knees and his fingertips were pressed together.

She had no idea what he wanted to discuss with her—maybe something happened with the divorce or he wanted to work on different skills when summer school ended for Hannah next week. This was Brock's conversation, his topic, so Casey waited quietly for him to begin talking.

"I didn't like you going out with Wyatt last night," Brock said quietly.

Of all the things Brock could have said, that wasn't what Casey was expecting. And, because she wasn't expecting it, she couldn't think of anything to say in return. So she stayed silent and listened.

"I'm still married." He glanced over at her for the briefest of moments.

She nodded her agreement.

"She's moved on with her life already," Brock said of Shannon.

That was new information he was sharing with her.

With a hollow laugh, he added, "She's already engaged. I didn't know someone could get engaged before they're divorced, but I guess it can happen."

Brock looked at her now. "Hannah doesn't know."

Casey swallowed hard a couple of times; her mouth had just gone completely dry. "I won't tell her."

"Thank you."

There was another break in the conversation before Brock went on to say, "I had been so focused on Shannon and the fact that *she* had moved on from our marriage that I didn't know that I had moved on, too."

Casey's eyes widened as they shifted to his profile.

Slowly, as the conversation progressed, her heartbeat was picking up pace, picking up pace…

"When I saw you go out the door last night with another man…" Brock kept his eyes locked onto the horizon. "I knew that I couldn't go another day without telling you how I feel…about you.

"You are such a good-hearted woman, Casey. You honestly are. Everyone loves you because you're just so kind to people."

He looked at her as he continued. "You always try to see the best in people or look on the bright side… Even when you aren't feeling well, you still try to find a silver lining."

"Some people find that to be super annoying," Casey said.

"Then I find them annoying." Brock was quick to jump to her defense. That was his first instinct—to protect those people he cared about the most. She was beginning to realize that *she* was now one of those people.

"You're so good with Hannah—she loves you."

"I love her, too."

Brock's daughter had become very important to her.

"You've become one of my best friends." The ranch foreman took her hand and held it gently in his. "But I want more."

Their eyes locked in a way that had never happened before. There was a trust there, a sense of security, and because of that foundation, they were able to be vulnerable with each other. Brock's eyes, the true windows to his soul, were open so she could see his heart—his intentions.

"Do you…want more…with me?" In that moment,

he was opening himself up to her—he was taking another shot at love after being badly hurt—and this spoke volumes about his character.

Casey squeezed his hand with her fingers to reassure him. "I do."

His shoulders dropped in what Casey could only describe in her mind as "relief" at her response. Her feelings for Brock had been growing steadily since the moment he had rescued her off that fence. But he had been understandably focused on his divorce from Shannon and raising his daughter, so she had pushed her feelings aside.

"But…" she added, "I think that we just need to take things real slow. You're still not through the divorce with Shannon—that's going to take a toll on you. And to layer a new relationship into the mix… I don't want to do anything that would hurt our friendship. Because your friendship has meant the world to me—it really has."

Brock gave her hand a quick kiss. "I agree."

His lunch break was over; it was time to let him get back to work so she could get back to her plan for the day—riding Gigi.

"Hey!" Casey climbed to the chapel step and waved her hand for Brock to come stand by her. "Now I'm as tall as you are."

Brock smiled at her affectionately.

"When's the last time you gave someone a piggyback ride?" She had her hands on her hips.

"I don't know—not since Hannah was young. Why?"

She made a circle with her finger. "Turn around, mountain man. I need a ride."

He looked at her like she had fallen off her rocker, but he did turn around.

Brock needed to lighten up and have a good time every now and again. And, if showing him a good time also included getting a piggyback ride down the hill? All the better for her.

It was easy to climb onto his back from her perch; she put her arms around his neck and he hooked his arms behind her knees.

"Where am I taking you?" he asked.

"Down the hill," she ordered him playfully. "Can you handle it?"

"Can I handle it?" he asked, feigning insult. "Just watch and learn."

Brock didn't walk to the hill; instead, he took off like a bull charging a red flag—head down and full steam ahead. She screamed in surprise and tightened her grip on his neck.

"Hold on! We're going for it now," he warned her.

She was amazed that a man his size could move that fast. He barely slowed down when they started down the hill. Casey, who had zero control in this situation, could only hold on and enjoy the ride. He wasn't going to drop her—she knew that. So she started to laugh—because it was fun. And because he had surprised her in a wonderful way.

At the bottom of the hill, Brock stopped and let Casey go. He was out of breath from a different type of exertion he was accustomed to doing from day to day. His eyes were shining and it was nice to see him smile the way he was smiling at her now—no reservations. Just pure happiness.

Casey, who didn't like anyone to have the upper

hand, decided to practice her self-defense training. Without any warning, she stepped on his instep and pushed on the spot on his body were his leg met his groin, and before the ranch foreman knew what was happening, he was sitting in the grass.

The reaction on his face was priceless. *Priceless!*

Casey held up her arms like Rocky Balboa and pranced around in a circle while she loudly hummed the Rocky theme song.

When she was done celebrating, she stood, hands on hips, triumphant. But it didn't last. Brock reached out with his long arms, grabbed her wrist and pulled her down beside him.

"Where'd you learn how to do that?" Brock asked her. "Not many people can say that they've gotten the better of me."

Casey made a karate chop in the air. "Taylor and I took a self-defense class."

They both started to laugh and it felt *right*. The sun was shining, the grass was soft, the sky was bright blue and she was having the time of her life with a man who was a great friend. And maybe…just maybe…*more*.

The next night, Casey and Brock sat together on the porch after Hannah had gone up to bed. Brock had Hercules in his lap—it was undeniable that the poodle had won the ranch foreman over. And it was a good sign to her that Hercules loved Brock in return.

"I talked to Shannon today."

Casey's heart gave the tiniest jump before resuming its regular rhythm.

"We've agreed on a settlement."

There had been this struggle between Brock and

Shannon, lurking beneath the surface, impacting Hannah and Brock and her in ways that were often indescribable. She could almost always tell when he had dealt with "California," as he put it, because his demeanor was so different afterward. As much as he tried to hide it and keep it separate from his life with Hannah, he wasn't a man who could easily paste a smile on his face and pretend like everything was peachy when it wasn't.

"Hannah will live with me during the school year. She'll live with Shannon during the summer. We'll rotate major holidays. Shannon gets Taj…"

Casey couldn't help it—she gasped at the thought of Brock losing his stallion.

"I will keep the house and give her a credit for half the value of the house, minus the value of Taj."

She reached out to hold on to his hand. "I'm so sorry about Taj, Brock. I know how much he means to you."

"I'll miss him," Brock acknowledged. "God knows I will. But I had to do what was best for Hannah. It took me a while to realize that I was holding on for all the wrong reasons. Letting go of Taj—I'm doing that for the right reason."

"Shannon will be here next week to take Hannah to California for the rest of the summer break. She'll pick up Taj and take him with them."

She squeezed his hand to comfort him. "I'll sign the mediation agreement, have it notarized—after that, we just wait for a court date so a judge can declare us officially divorced."

There was pure bitterness in Brock's voice when he said the words *officially divorced*. She knew that Brock *wanted* to be ready to move on, but his emotions were going to be all over the place for a while—that was normal. It was also perfectly normal for her to move with caution with this man and protect her heart.

Chapter Twelve

A week after Brock announced that he was moving forward with his divorce, Shannon arrived with a shiny black Silverado truck and a shiny black horse trailer. When Brock's soon-to-be ex-wife showed up, Casey was sitting in one of the rocking chairs answering emails on her computer. It was a bit awkward because Brock hadn't returned from taking Hannah to a doctor's appointment in Helena.

Shannon stepped out of the truck looking like she had stepped right out of a *Vogue* magazine shoot. Her long, flowing, perfectly highlighted, brandy-colored hair framed her undeniably beautiful heart-shaped face. She was six feet tall, slender but with nice curves in the right places. Honestly, Shannon was the kind of woman you assume doesn't exist in real life. And yet, there she was—it was like spotting a unicorn.

Shannon slid her mirrored aviator sunglasses to the top of her head before she looked around the ranch. Casey could read her expression as easily as she could read a Dr. Seuss book—*what a dump*.

"Hi there!" Shannon walked over to the house. "You must be Casey."

Casey put her computer on the seat next to her so she could stand up to greet Hannah's mother.

"Guilty." Casey smiled a friendly smile and offered Shannon her hand.

They shook hands and then Shannon looked around again with the slightest disapproving shake of her head, and said, "I was so hoping to see Brock take initiative with this place. It's sad when people don't live up to their full potential."

Casey had to bite her tongue—literally bite her tongue. She had promised herself that she *was not* going to get in the middle of this divorce. Yes, she was a friend of Brock's, and they were considering exploring a deeper relationship, but to get sucked into the muck that was the end of a marriage? No, thank you.

On the other hand, it pissed her off that Shannon was putting Brock down. The man had an outstanding work ethic.

"Brock and Hannah should be back from Helena soon—do you want something to drink? I just made a fresh batch of sun tea."

Shannon stared down at her. "Well, isn't that *sweet* of you. I guess I'll just have to get used to a stranger inviting me into my own home."

After she threw out the barb, Shannon laughed to signal that she was "just kidding." But Casey had been in the company of catty women before, and this kitty cat had very sharp claws.

"And the surprises just keep coming," Shannon said when she walked into the house. She walked straight into the living room, looking at the new wood floors and the freshly painted walls and molding.

Hannah's mom turned around and smiled a stiff smile at her. "Well, you must be a little miracle worker, Casey. I could never get Brock to change a lightbulb in this place if it'd burned out."

Casey refused to let the woman bait her. "He did it for Hannah."

"Now, that's the Brock I know." Shannon accepted the glass of tea Casey offered to her. "Anything for Hannah."

Casey didn't like the way the ranch felt after Hannah and Taj left. There was a gaping hole left by them, a vacuum that couldn't be filled. Brock told her again and again that he was "fine," but the ranch foreman looked like part of his heart had been ripped out of his chest. There was sadness in him now, so much sadness that he refused to give a voice. Instead, he was stuffing it down and going on about his business as if nothing was wrong and everything was the same. As far Brock was concerned—he was fine—just fine.

Brooding had never been her MO and it was hard for her to handle it in other people. She was more of a "pick yourself up, dust yourself off and get the heck on with it" kind of gal. Wanting to escape the black mood that was currently occupying Brock's ranch, Casey went into town to spend the day with Taylor and Sophia and the four little ones.

The seven of them walked to the nearby park. Casey carried her niece, who had on a pretty sunflower dress and a matching yellow headband. As far as Casey was concerned, she was the cutest baby on the planet.

"I can't wait to have my own," Casey said as she put Penny in the baby swing.

"If you'd married Scott," Taylor reminded her, "you'd be living in the suburbs with a couple of kids."

"How long ago was Scott?" Sophia was kneeling by her son, Danny, tying his shoelace in a double knot.

"I don't know." Casey gave her niece a little push and loved to see her smile as she swung closer and then swung farther away. "Five years ago?"

"He was such a nice guy," Taylor reminisced. "He got along with Mom—*impossible*—and Dad recommended him as an intern at the firm."

Taylor said directly to Sophia, "And he was crazy about Casey. He wanted babies, she wanted babies... he gave her a ring, they set a date and then..."

Sophia kept a keen eye on her children, who were playing a few yards away. "Cold feet?"

"Frozen is more like it." Casey laughed. "I felt horrible about breaking off our engagement. I really did. But it didn't matter how sweet he was, or attentive he was, or how perfectly he fit into my plan...we just weren't *compatible* in the bedroom department."

"Oh, no." Sophia's face registered complete understanding. "That *has* to work. It's not everything, but it has to be *something*."

"Exactly." Casey made a face at her sister. "See— Sophia understands."

"I didn't say it didn't matter... I just don't think you should throw away a perfect guy over it. They have retreats—don't they, Sophia? You go out into the woods and hit drums and dance in circles naked…"

Sophia, who was a trained psychologist, smiled at the thought. "That's not really my area of expertise…"

"It was really hard to break up with him," Casey admitted. "I cried. He cried. It was a whole scene."

The breakup with Scott had really made her gun-shy about getting into another relationship. She dated here and there, but the men she attracted just weren't *right*. But she could never pinpoint exactly what was missing.

"I tell you what, the ranch seems really strange without Hannah around. It's been really tough on Brock."

The minute she brought up Brock to her sister, Taylor's body language changed and the silent message she sent was: *I don't want to talk about him.*

But she *did* want to talk about Brock. She saw a future with the ranch foreman—she saw a future with the family she had been craving for so long. Somehow, this mess with Clint and Brock was going to have to be sorted out.

"How have you been feeling? Did you ever get in touch with that doctor?" Taylor was consistent and changed the subject right on schedule.

"No," Casey replied. "I've been feeling okay. I still have a twinge of pain here and there, but that's to be expected with endometriosis."

"Dr. Hall is the best gynecologist on the planet," Sophia chimed in. "I swear that woman knows her way around a vagina. I think she's flat-out amazing. She warms the speculum, too, so that's a bonus."

"For sure she gets kudos for the warm speculum. *But* if I don't need to go…then I'm not gonna volun-

teer to have a stranger poke around in my nether re-
gions just for the fun of it," Casey said. "Thank you,
but *no thank you*."

Back on the ranch, she was surprised to see Brock
home so early. She stood by the VW for a moment—
she had been giving Brock his space and he had been
taking it. But something in her gut told her that, as his
friend, enough was enough. She put Hercules on the
ground so he could greet his girlfriend, Lady.

"Hi, Ladybug." Casey gave the Lab a scratch on her
neck, which was her favorite spot.

Brock was at the kitchen table; on the table was an
open bottle of some sort of alcohol and a single glass.

"What's the occasion?" Casey asked him.

Brock looked up at her as if he had just noticed that
she was there. His shirt was unbuttoned and his hair
was mussed. It seemed that he had already indulged
quite a bit—his eyes were glassy.

"Here…" Brock reached behind him to grab a glass
from the drain. He slammed the glass down on the
table, pulled the cork out of the bottle and poured her
a drink. "Join me."

He poured himself another drink—it was a sloppy
pour and liquor sloshed over the rim and onto the table.

The ranch foreman held out his glass to toast her.
"Congratulate me."

"For…?"

"I am—" Brock pointed at his chest "—a free man."

"Wait a minute…" Casey sat down and put her glass
down. "You're divorced? How could it have possibly
happened that fast?"

Brock tipped his head back to polish off every bit

of liquor in his glass. "Well, funny story. Shannon's fiancé, Carl... His father skis every winter in Montana with a law school buddy of his, who—you guessed it—is a judge in Helena. The father asks his friend for a favor, and since everything's already been settled through mediation, the judge fast-tracked our case. Shannon's decided to keep the name McAllister and hyphenate after she gets married. She's shooting for a June wedding next year so Hannah can attend."

Now *she* felt like she needed a drink. Brock being married had always been a reason to keep him safely in the friend zone—now that he was a free man, the dynamic between them would undoubtedly change.

"What is this?" Casey sniffed the alcohol.

"Cognac," Brock told her. "Good cognac. Sorry I don't have the proper glasses."

Casey held out her glass. "What does one toast to in a situation like this? Happy divorce?"

Brock poured himself another. "That'll do."

They touched glasses. Brock downed his and she took a healthy sip of hers. He slammed his glass down and then drummed his fingers on the table.

Casey looked up to find Brock staring at her.

"What?" she asked him when he just continued to stare at her as if he didn't recognize her.

"Are you my friend, Casey?"

"Yes," she told him. "Of course I am. Why?"

"Because I intend to get drunk tonight and I might show my ass, if you know what I mean. If you're my friend—you won't judge me."

"I'm not going to judge you," she reassured him. "I'll even pour the drinks for you. But you've got to make me a promise, Brock..."

"I'm not sure I'm in any condition to make a promise, but go ahead…"

"After tonight? You've got to snap out of it and start enjoying your life again. God knows Shannon isn't sitting around crying in her beer."

Brock raised a brow at her. "Now—that was cold."

Casey leaned forward. "I know—did I go too far? I was trying to motivate you."

"No." Brock surprised her by chuckling a little. "I like your style."

Casey sipped on her one glass of what turned out to be very expensive vintage Hennessey cognac that Brock had been saving for a special occasion. Brock polished off the entire bottle. She kept him company and she was there for him to lean on when he needed a guiding hand to get him safely from the table to the couch.

"Why are you so good to me?" he asked her when she helped him pull off his boots.

"Because—" Casey handed him a large glass of water and some aspirin "—you're my friend and I love you."

Brock popped the aspirin into his mouth before he guzzled the water. "I love you."

One minute she was standing upright and the next thing she realized, she was half sitting, half lying on top of a now reclining Brock. He had reached out, scooped her up like she didn't weigh an ounce, and he had her in a bear hug with his face buried in her hair.

"You smell good," he murmured drunkenly. "Lemony."

"That's the dishwashing soap."

"Mmmmm." This was the only response she got out of him.

"Brock? I need to get up now."

This wasn't sexual—it wasn't a come-on—he was cuddling her like she was a life-size teddy bear. Then she heard him snoring.

"Really?" Casey started to wiggle her body in earnest and managed to wriggle free of his heavy arms.

She got the blanket off the back of the couch to drape over him. Casey stared down at this man who had become so important to her. She'd told him she loved him and she'd meant it. She did. No matter if they went any further with each other—that was another subject entirely—but as a person, as a friend, as a man, she loved him.

"Lord have mercy, Brock." Casey breathed in deeply and then sighed it out heavily. "We have got to get you back in your own bed."

"Good morning!" Casey poked a snoring Brock with her finger.

The man must have really tied one on because she had been banging around in the kitchen for an hour and the only time he'd moved was to turn over with an annoyed grunt.

"Coffee." She tugged on his beard. *"Coffee!"*

"Blast it, Casey! I heard you! Coffee! I heard you!"

"If you heard me," she said sweetly with sarcasm laced in, "then get up! Day's a'wastin', my friend, and we have a full agenda."

"It's my day off." He covered his eyes with his arm.

"I know," she told him. "It's your day off and we have a lot to do. How's that hangover?"

"Not too bad. Considering."

"I made you drink water before you passed out."
Casey put some scrambled eggs on a plate with toast.
"Come eat some breakfast."

Brock ate a couple helpings of eggs, three pieces of
buttered toast, a glass of orange juice and two cups of
coffee. The man could really pack it away, even after
a night of drinking.

While she washed the dishes, he went upstairs to
take a much-needed shower and change into clean
clothes. He looked refreshed and clean—his shirt was
tucked in and his hair was combed back off his face.
The man smelled good again.

"Now what do you have up your sleeve?" Brock
had sat back down at the table and was watching her
put away the dishes that had dried in the drying rack
overnight.

Casey shut the cabinet door. "We're going into town
so you can pick out a new mattress."

When he didn't say "yeah" or "nay" she stood in
front of him and asked, "No objection?"

He shook his head. "You slapped some sense into
me last night. I've got to get the heck on with it. A new
mattress is a fine place to start."

"Huh…" She liked to see him taking the bull by
the horns, so to speak. "If that's how you really feel,
then you shouldn't object to one thing I want to do."

He raised his eyebrows questioningly.

"Brock—I say this with love, I really do, but you
have to let me trim your beard."

Brock rubbed his hand over his scruffy beard. "You
don't like the beard?"

"No. I didn't say that. I like it actually. And beards

are in now. But I think we need to take it down a couple of notches from Neanderthal."

His long legs were stretched out in front of him and she was standing in the space between his calves. He looked at her face with such admiration that it made her cheeks feel hot, like she was actually blushing.

"You are mighty pretty, Casey Brand."

"Don't change the subject."

He hooked his pointer finger in the loop of her jeans. "I'm not. If you want to trim my beard, you are welcome to have your way with me."

Brock tugged her forward so he could put his hands on either side of her hips. Now that he was a free man, he was very comfortable touching her. She wasn't sure she was as comfortable as he was, but on the other hand, she didn't have any desire to pull away from him. It would just take her a minute to get used to this sudden shift in their boundaries.

"You told me you loved me last night." He was staring into her eyes so intently.

She had to look away—it was like he was trying to read every word written on her soul. "And I meant it."

"Hey…" He wanted her to shift her eyes back to his. "I meant it, too."

"Could we just…slow down for a minute?" She pushed away from him.

Brock let her go. "I've wanted to be able to touch you for a long time now."

She crossed her arms in front of her body. "I know. And I respect the fact that you wanted to finish with one relationship before you started another. That's something I really respect about you. But it hasn't even been twenty-four hours yet."

"Okay." The one word was all he said.

"I just need time to process, I think."

He reached for her hand and gave it a reassuring squeeze. "So what do you want to do first? Mattress or beard?"

They were back in safe territory now, which suited her.

"I never say no to shopping. So, mattress first, beard later."

Shopping in Helena, Montana, was the polar opposite experience to shopping her favorite haunts in Chicago. Chicago was teeming with choices and price points—a shopper's paradise. Helena on the other hand? Not so much. However, there did seem to be quite a few places to shop for mattresses in Helena. Brock had Wi-Fi in his truck, so she researched stores while he drove them into town.

"Okay—I'm leaning toward Macy's because they're familiar. But I have to tell you, Mattress Madness is tickling my fancy. It's a stove and mattress combo store."

"Good deals there."

She raised her eyebrows at him. "You knew I was being facetious, right?"

Brock gave her a quick little wink. "Yes, dear."

When she had originally had the thought to take Brock to buy a new mattress, it never occurred to her that she would be helping him make a selection. At least not in the way he wanted her to help him.

Brock had been lying on one of the higher-end mattresses with his arms at his sides and his eyes closed.

"Well?" she asked him impatiently. "What do you think?"

"I've been waiting on you." His eyes still closed, he patted the empty spot beside him. "Give it a whirl."

"What I think doesn't matter. It's *your* mattress."

Brock opened his eyes. "Down the road a piece, you're going to be sleeping in it with me, so you've got to tell me if you like it or not."

Casey looked around to see if the salesman helping them was in earshot. "That's putting the cart *way* before the horse, don't you think?"

"No." He patted the empty spot again. "I've got a real strong feeling about me and you."

Chapter Thirteen

She didn't necessarily agree with him that she was picking out a mattress for *them* as opposed to *him*, but Brock refused to get up until she gave him her honest opinion. Soon, because she had a strong opinion about everything shopping, she was trying out all of the mattresses with him. Brock purchased a California king that would fit the bed frame in the master bedroom upstairs and then he shadowed Casey as she wove her way through the misses and junior clothing department, through accessories, around the perfume and makeup counters into the shoe department.

I'll just try on a few pairs turned into Casey happily surrounded by a wonderful fort of boot boxes. Brock sat across from her, his big frame stuffed into the standard-issue shoe-department chair. He couldn't be comfortable, but to his credit, the man just sat there scrolling through his phone while she tried on one style of boot after another after another. She lived on a teacher's salary, so she knew that once she did have a family the shoe obsession would have to be tamped down—but as she didn't have kids at the moment, shoes were part of her family.

She left Macy's with three new pairs of fabulous boots—one ankle boot to fill the empty void left by her ruined Jimmy Choo boots, may they rest in peace, and two pairs of knee-high boots, one black and one tan and brown ombre. Brock carried her bags for her while she chatted happily about stumbling upon such a great shoe sale. It wasn't right—she knew it wasn't right—but shopping always gave her a wonderful shot of endorphins.

Brock opened the truck door for her and she climbed up into the cab of his truck. She was still talking about their shopping excursion when he cranked the engine.

"Aren't you happy that we found a new mattress for you?"

The ranch foreman nodded.

"Yeah—me, too." She sighed, pleased with how the morning had worked out for the both of them. She was on a talkative streak, which could be attributed to the new boot cache in the backseat *and* the giant high-octane coffee she had power guzzled for energy prior to her search-and-rescue mission through the shoe department.

The most she was able to get out of Brock was a couple of grunts and nods.

"You aren't saying much," she finally complained.

He glanced over at her as they came to a red light. "I'm listening to you."

"A conversation usually includes two people." She held up two fingers. "I say something, then you say something... Where are we going?"

He wasn't taking the road back to the ranch.

"I made an appointment to get a haircut and a shave. You wanted me to get that taken care of, didn't you?"

Casey turned her body toward Brock—the man never stopped surprising her. He really didn't.

Bone's Barber Shop was the next stop on their "just divorced" victory lap. When the barber asked Brock what he wanted to have done, the ranch foreman had nodded to her and said, "Whatever she wants."

Casey had to admit that she was mesmerized by the slow transformation of Brock McAllister from a mild-mannered mountain man to a straight-up hunk. The barber started with the shaggy hair. Brock's hair had grown in unruly waves down to his shoulders, but when the barber was finished cutting, the rancher only had an inch of hair on top. The barber then cleaned up the line around Brock's ears, ears that Casey couldn't remember seeing before, and cleaned up the edge of his hair just at the nape of the neck.

The beard—a beard that could require its own zip code—was tackled next. The hot towel came off Brock's face and the straight razor came out. As per her request, the barber kept the beard, but trimmed it down considerably. Totally trusting the process, or maybe he just wasn't concerned all that much by his appearance in general, Brock had his eyes closed while the barber worked with a straight-edge razor and shaving lotion beneath his chin and neck.

Brock had almost dozed off when he felt the barber wipe down his face with a lukewarm towel; the barber applied aftershave and then sat him upright. He opened his eyes and stared at his reflection in the mirror—he didn't look like himself anymore. At least not the man he had been for the last several years. His eyes sought out, and found, Casey's eyes in the mirror. He was hoping she would look pleased, but her reaction was far more gratifying. It was as if she were seeing him, truly seeing him, for the first time. Perhaps she was.

"Do I meet with your approval, Ms. Brand?" he asked her.

She walked around to the front of his chair, surprise and, yes, *attraction*, there for him to easily see in her wide green eyes.

"You are handsome," she told him plainly. And he knew she meant it.

He paid the barber a generous tip then asked the redhead of his affection out to lunch. It felt like their first date…even though they had been meeting at the chapel every week this summer, this was the first time they were "going out" together. He felt proud, very proud, to have Casey walking beside him. And now, with his new image, he hoped she was proud to be walking beside him.

"I'm am *so* hungry!" Casey sat opposite Brock.

He had brought her to his favorite pizza spot— Bullman's Wood Fired Pizza. The pizza oven was right there for all the customers to see—and the name wasn't false advertisement, either—a wood-burning fire heated the pizza oven.

"It smells so good in here." Casey's stomach, which had been rumbling before, started to hurt from the hunger.

She scoured the menu and decided that she had to

be adventurous and try the Bitterroot. She'd never eaten a pizza with the interesting combination of pistachios, red onions, rosemary, mozzarella, olive oil and sea salt. Brock ordered the Bitterroot for her and the Crazy Mountain for himself and added two bottles of Montana-made cider.

"What should we toast to today?" Casey asked him. "To freedom?"

Brock stared at her so intently that it made her squirm in her chair.

"I don't want my freedom," he told her. "I want to be with you."

"Brock…" she said gently. "I think it's too soon. You've only been divorced for one day."

"That's true," he agreed with her. "But I've been separated for years."

She wanted to change the subject. She had always liked to keep things light and upbeat—and this conversation was heading into territory that made her uncomfortable. Some, like her sister, would call her commitment-phobic. She had diagnosed herself as chronically cautious with her heart.

He must have read the resistance on her face and in her body language, because his next words were designed specifically to make her laugh and smile. And they worked.

"How about this? Let's toast to the buy-one-get-one-half-off shoe sale at Macy's."

Casey laughed and willingly held out her cider bottle. "You're a very quick study, aren't you, cowboy? Cheers to that!"

She tried to pay her portion of the bill, but Brock wouldn't hear of it. Casey couldn't believe how much pizza she had stuffed into her face. And she said as much to Brock when he climbed into the driver's seat.

"Look at this…" Casey pulled up her shirt and showed him her belly. "I ate so much of that pizza that I actually have a food baby."

"Not too many women will put food away like you do."

She frowned at him. "I think you meant that as a compliment…?"

"Of course I did."

"I've always been hyper as all get out. I burn through my calories and need to fuel right back up again. I usually go up and down about ten pounds—so I have two different wardrobes in my closet—but it's not my weight that gives me trouble, it's the cellulite. It just shows up, unannounced, now that I'm in my thirties. It's very annoying."

Brock was smiling at her minidiatribe about the woes of cellulite.

"That was the cider talking." Casey laughed. "I have no idea how my cellulite entered the conversation."

"I like to listen to you talk," Brock told her. "Today is a good day."

That day, the first official day of Brock being a free and clear man, was the beginning of a new chapter in the evolution of her relationship with the ranch foreman. His resolve, his focus and his quiet persistence on the matter of their future eroded most of her resistance. His appeal to her now, an appeal that had always been about who he was as a man—who he was as a father and a protector—had shifted. His makeover allowed her to see him in an entirely new light. He had always been hypermasculine and burly in his appearance—which wasn't repellent by any means—but the short hair and the groomed beard had transformed his face. She could see his teeth when he smiled, including the bottom two teeth that crossed just a little, which she now found endearing. She could see his eyes—clear eyes that admired her and had nothing to hide.

Over breakfast, she found herself staring at him. On their frequent rides together, she found herself staring at him. At the dinner table, more staring. He was so handsome to her eyes. So handsome. Inside and out. The real Brock had been hidden behind all of that hair for years.

Every morning, after breakfast, Brock would always ask her, "Are you going to meet me at the chapel today?"

In the beginning, they would plan a picnic at the chapel one time a week—but that wasn't enough for Brock anymore. He wanted her to meet him at the chapel every day. At the start of this new routine, she felt as if she were doing it mostly for Brock. Over time, she began to realize how important those picnics at the chapel were to her.

"You've got your hands full! Do you need a hand?"

Casey had been so intent on getting the picnic basket, Ladybug the Labrador *and* Hercules the all-time greatest poodle from the vintage VW up to the chapel, that she hadn't noticed the young cowboy tending to one of the mares in the foaling barn. She had discovered the short cut through the barn only last week.

"Wyatt Williams!" Casey stopped in her tracks to give her startled, racing heart a chance to recover. "*Why* do you always *do* that to me?"

Wyatt was hanging his arms over the stall gate, grinning at her as he always did. "Do what?"

"Scare the living daylights out of me! That's what!"

Wyatt came out of the stall to stand next to her in the barn aisle. "I don't mean to."

"I know. I know." She let him off the hook. Wyatt didn't have a mean, or serious, bone in his body. He was like an overgrown playful puppy.

"Let me give you a hand." Wyatt reached for the basket.

Casey didn't know how Brock would react to seeing Wyatt walking her up to their picnic spot. On the other hand, her hands were too full and there was a pretty steep hill to climb up to the chapel.

"All right." She handed him the basket while she managed Lady's leash and Hercules's carrier.

"I haven't see you in a while," the cowboy said. "You settling into fifty-three okay?"

"Very funny." She smiled at him.

She hadn't seen Wyatt since he had taken her dancing on her birthday. They'd texted a couple of times, but she knew that he was having fun and playing the field, and would get bored pursuing her without results.

"I didn't know you were Brock's girl. I wouldn't have taken you dancin' if I'd known that."

"I wasn't Brock's girl then."

He looked down at her with that perfectly symmetrical, chiseled, golden face. "But you are Brock's girl now."

The sound of that made her smile again, but this time it was a shyer, more self-conscious smile.

"Yes." She nodded her head. "I am Brock's girl now."

* * *

Brock had been thinking about this day for weeks; today was the day that he was going to kiss her. And not the kiss on the cheek that she had been holding him to for far too long. He had been wooing Casey Brand slowly and gentlemanly so he wouldn't spook her. He'd spent enough time with her now to figure a few things out—Casey wanted to have a husband and a family, but she was scared to death of taking a chance and risking failure. They had held hands and snuggled on the couch. They had gone for long, romantic rides and picnics at the chapel. But whenever he got close to going in for that first kiss, he always ended up holding Hercules instead. Casey could *sense* that the all-important, barrier-breaking kiss was upon them and she would find a reason to exit stage left. He didn't know how he had been maneuvered into this corner—a teacup poodle was regularly blocking his romantic mojo. How could something so tiny cause him so much trouble?

"Hi!" Casey called out to him breathlessly as she reached the top of the hill. "Wyatt was kind enough to help me."

Brock covered the distance between them in a few long strides. "I've got it from here. Thank you, Wyatt."

Wyatt handed the basket to the ranch foreman, tipped his hat to both of them and then jogged down the hill and back to the foaling barn.

"Well, that was a lot more civil than I thought it would be," Casey said of the interaction between the two cowboys.

Brock took the blanket out of the basket and spread it out in their favorite spot. "I had a talk with him."

Casey was about to sit down but snapped upright instead. "You *talked* with him? Like you staked your claim?"

"We talked."

Her hands were on her hips. "Well, that was mighty 1890s of you."

"Quit your bellyachin', woman," Brock teased her, "and fix me my lunch."

They unpacked the picnic—she had brought a brand-new, giant-sized Milk-Bone for Lady and a miniature-sized Milk-Bone for Hercules. Once everything was unpacked and the four of them were settled in, Brock turned on one of her favorite classical pieces.

"What kind of wedding do you want to have?" Brock had finished his food and was lying on his side petting Lady. Hercules was sitting on the top of Brock's boot, so the ranch foreman was careful not to move his legs and launch the mini-poodle.

Casey wiped her mouth with a napkin. "Small. Intimate."

She hadn't always dreamed of her wedding like many of her friends had—but she had dreamed of the children who would follow the wedding.

"I think I'd like to marry you right here," Brock told her. "In this chapel."

In her mind, she saw herself, in a simple antique white lace dress, standing hand in hand with Brock, inside the chapel. And the thought didn't scare her.

"I think the chapel would be the perfect place to get married," she agreed.

He reached for her hand. "If we kept it small, Hannah would be able to attend."

Casey rubbed her finger over the nail of his thumb. "I miss her."

"So do I."

Their minds turned to Hannah and neither of them spoke for a couple of minutes. Then Brock brought up the subject that had been on his mind all morning.

"I'm going to kiss you today, Casey."

His comment had shifted the topic pretty dramatically and it made her laugh. He could never do anything in the conventional way.

"I'm giving you fair warning," he added.

"Why do you think that I need fair warning?"

He gave her a look. "You know why."

She did know why—every time Brock had even remotely acted like he was going to kiss her, she managed to find a reason to stop him. She had never been a fan of the first kiss—it was built up so much and what if she hated it? It was hard to imagine marrying someone you didn't like to kiss. That one kiss could ruin everything. And she hadn't been ready to risk it.

"Okay." Casey made a decision; she stood up and held out her hand to Brock. "Come on."

Brock smiled up at her. "Where are you taking me?"

"I'm going to kiss you." She shook her hand for him to take it. "Are you coming or not?"

"Sorry, buddy, but you need to stay here." Brock picked Hercules up off his boot and put him on the picnic blanket.

When the ranch foreman was standing, Casey took his hand in hers and led him decisively over to the chapel steps.

"You stay down there," she told him while she walked up the first couple of steps. She turned around, and now that she was standing on the chapel steps, they were almost the same height.

Without hesitation, Casey put her hands on either side of Brock's face and pressed her lips to his.

It wasn't a deep kiss, but it was the kind of kiss that left an impression. She liked the feel of his beard beneath her fingertips and the firmness of his lips as they were pressed against hers.

"There!" she said when the kiss was over. "Now that's done."

Brock seemed glad that they had broken that barrier. But she could see that he wasn't satisfied with just one short kiss.

"You're beautiful to me." Brock pulled her closer. "I love you, Casey."

And then he kissed her. His way. Slow. Deep. Sensual.

He held her so close that she could feel his heart beating against her breast. The first kiss confirmed that she loved him. The second kiss convinced her that she wanted to make love with him.

When they came up for a breath, Brock kissed her forehead and her cheeks and her neck.

"Tell me that you'll marry me here one day, Casey," he said into her neck.

She hugged him tightly, resting her head on his chest, so she could still feel his heart that was beating so strongly for her.

"I promise that I will marry you here one day."

She said it and she meant it.

Brock let out a whoop and tossed his hat in the air. He picked her up off the step and swung her in a circle until they were both a little dizzy.

They were laughing and out of breath when he stopped swinging her and let her slide down his body until her feet were safely on the ground.

Now that he could kiss her—now that she was willing to *let him* kiss her—that's all he wanted to do. There, in the sunlight, in front of the Bent Tree chapel and beneath the bright blue expanse of the Montana sky, the ranch foreman kissed the woman he knew would one day be his bride.

Chapter Fourteen

The decision to leave her bed that night and go to Brock wasn't difficult to make. The full moon was so crisp and clear in the starless sky and cast a glowing yellow light through the large loft window. She hadn't been able to sleep and she knew why. Brock was alone in the upstairs bedroom while she was alone in her bed—and it didn't need to be that way. They didn't need to be alone anymore. Not when they had each other.

Casey left the loft with poodle in hand—she quietly entered the house, dropped Hercules off with his girlfriend and then used the flashlight on her phone to light her footsteps up to the second floor. The same moonlight that had lit the loft was streaming into Brock's bedroom and dancing across the bed where her man was sleeping.

She stood by the empty side of the bed and pulled her braid over her shoulder to pull the hair tie from the bottom of the braid. She slowly unbraided her hair until it was swinging loose down her back to the top of her derriere. Brock was snoring softly, lying on his side, unaware that she was in the room with him. He wouldn't reject her. He had been patiently waiting for her. Casey pulled her nightie off and dropped it on the floor beside her bare feet. She hooked her thumbs on her silky bikini panties, slid them down over her hips, down to her ankles and then stepped free of them. Now she was completely naked in the moonlight. Vulnerable as she had never dared to allow herself to be before.

"Brock." Casey said her love's name.

Brock heard his name as if he were hearing it in the distance—in the fog—so soft that he thought he was dreaming it. When he opened his eyes to find an angel with pale, pale skin covered only by beautiful strands of red hair, he thought he had imagined her. That he had wanted Casey to come to him so badly that his mind had manufactured her likeness out of thin air.

"Brock."

She said his name again and this time he knew that this was not a dream—she was real. Casey had finally come to him as he had willed her to do in his mind so many nights.

"Are you sure you're ready for this?" His voice was husky from a mixture of sleep and need.

He saw her nod her head—he saw a small smile on her pretty pink lips. He pulled the covers back for her. As she walked the short distance to the bed, he soaked in the image of her ethereal body—so much softer and feminine in its nakedness. Her breasts were naturally rounded, not large, but perfectly shaped. The nipples—they had grown hard in his mouth. At the apex of her thighs there was a triangle of red curls. He wanted to bury his face there and taste her sweetness.

And then she was in his arms. Her skin was chilled from the night air—he covered her with the blanket and wrapped her tightly in his arms. She was shivering. He would have to go slow—it had been a long time in between lovers for both of them.

"This is it for me, Casey." Brock curled his body around hers and kissed the back of her neck. "I love you."

Casey responded by kissing his hand. "I love you."

When her body was warmed, Brock let go of her just long enough to discard his underwear. She turned in his arms and they pressed their bodies together, for the warmth and the comfort. Her skin, so smooth and soft, was everything his skin wasn't. He was hairy and rough—she felt like silk all over.

He kissed her, slowly so he could enjoy it and deeply so she was reminded of things to come. She tasted minty, like toothpaste, and she moved her hips into his body as he deepened the kiss.

She gasped the sweetest, sexiest gasp when he flicked his tongue across the hard tip of her nipple. He held her breast firmly in his hand and sucked her nipple until she dug her fingernails into his shoulder.

"I've wanted to touch you like this for so long."

Casey reached between them and wrapped her fingers around his erection.

Brock's body shuddered at the touch of her hand—it had been years since a woman had touched him like that.

His need had been so great, for such a long time, that he had been afraid he wouldn't be able to love her the way he wanted to on their first night. For weeks, he had been releasing himself so he could last long enough to bring her to climax. If he hadn't been preparing his body, that first touch of her hand may have been his rapid, untimely undoing. Especially since they had agreed that condoms weren't required—Casey had received a long-lasting birth control shot and neither of them had been sexually active in several years. Without a condom to reduce sensation, he could climax before they even got started.

"Are you okay?" he asked his love.

"I'm happy," she said so quietly. "I love you."

Brock worried that his hands were too big or too rough as he ran his fingers down her belly and along her muscular thighs. Her legs had grown so strong from a summer of riding—he could feel the power in them just as he felt the satin of her skin. He slipped his fingers between her thighs—so warm, so wet, so ready for him. He wanted to taste that warmth between her beautiful thighs, but he knew that he had to take his time with Casey. There would be time for more exploring and experimenting later. For now, he just wanted her to be comfortable in his arms, in his bed. He wanted her to adjust to his weight on top of her and the feel of having his body filling hers.

Casey started to tug on his arm, pulling him toward her. He lifted himself up and moved between her thighs. Brock held himself above her—he wanted to look down on her; what a pretty vision she created with her ivory skin against his dark sheets and her hair spread across his pillows.

She reached down between them to guide him. So tight. So tight and warm and slick. He slid his body into hers and they moaned in unison. Her body completely enveloped him; she felt like nothing he'd ever experienced before. Their bodies fit together so perfectly—it didn't make sense, but it didn't have to.

Brock lowered his body until his chest was pressed against her breasts. He slid his arms beneath their bodies so he could hold her even tighter against his chest. She mirrored him, wrapping her arms and legs around his body—drawing him in deeper and deeper.

"Am I too heavy for you?" he asked when he heard her gasp.

She gasped again and he lifted up his body just in time to see how the woman he loved looked when she climaxed. He stopped moving his body so she could set the rhythm, so she could use his body to prolong the orgasm. When she cried out again, and he felt the wetness of her release on his thighs, he couldn't hold himself back any longer.

"God, God, God…" Brock's body shuddered and his arms tightened around Casey.

After a minute of Brock laying his full weight on top of her, Casey pushed on his shoulder with a languid laugh.

"*Now* you're too heavy for me."

He carefully disconnected their bodies then rolled onto his back. "Come over here with me."

Casey curled up next to her bear of a man—she rested her arm on his shoulder, her hand on his furry chest, and put her leg over his thick thigh.

"Mmm." She closed her eyes with a contented sigh. "We're really good at that."

Brock laughed and kissed her on her damp forehead. "We are good at that."

"I'm going to sleep now, okay?" Casey turned over onto her other side.

"Me, too." He turned with her.

Brock shaped his body to hers, his arm beneath her body and holding her across her chest. "I love you."

Casey tilted her head back so she could kiss him one last time. "I love you, sweet man."

That first night of loving sparked a wild week of lovemaking. The more comfortable Casey became with him, the more risks she wanted to take. In fact, he wasn't usually the aggressor in the sexual arena— she was. She would come up behind him when he was cooking, unzip his pants and stimulate him with her hands. He could count several ruined meals because he wasn't about to pass up an invitation like that from Casey. She also enjoyed making love in the morning. He'd wake up with her mouth getting him hard and ready. Those were his favorite mornings—groggy with a raging hard-on and the love of his life climbing on top of him. That lovemaking was always sensual and slow, with Casey covering his body with hers, both of them beneath the covers. He'd wake up every morning that way if he could.

They loved each other so much that their body parts were sore—but it didn't matter. They couldn't keep their hands off each other and they didn't *want* to keep their hands off each other. And that included when they were supposed be showering to go out.

Instead of waiting for her turn in the shower, Casey opened the shower door and stepped inside. Brock was standing with his back to her, rinsing the soap off the front part of his body. She ran her hands across his back and started to lick little droplets of water from his skin.

"Mmm. That feels nice, baby."

Brock turned around so they could hug each other while the hot water ran over their bodies. It didn't take long for her to feel his body start to respond. She leaned back and smiled up at him.

"Look at what you do to me—all you have to do is touch me."

Casey lowered her body down, running her hands over his stomach.

"I need to lose a couple of pounds," he said about his less-than-flat stomach.

Casey put her finger to her lips. "Shhh."

When she took him in her mouth, he reached out to steady himself by putting his hands flat on either side of the shower. The hotness of the shower, the hotness of her mouth—he knew what she wanted from him— she wanted him hard and ready to love her. And that's exactly what she got.

Brock lifted Casey up into his arms, walked her to the edge of the shower so her back was pressed against the cool tile and while he was kissing her, he was sliding her down onto his shaft.

"Ah…" Casey dropped her head back as he kissed the water from her neck.

"It's too damn slippery in here." Brock laughed. "I need to put something on the floor to keep my feet from sliding."

Casey wiped the water off his face and kissed his lips. "Take me to the bed."

Their bodies dripping puddles of water on the floor, Brock carried her to the bed and laid her back with her legs hanging off the side. Still standing, he guided himself back into her body and pushed her knees to her chest. They had loved each other enough that they could look into each other's eyes as they made love— and this was an entirely new position to enjoy.

Casey arched her back to take him deeper and then he hit something that hurt. She pulled away and held out her hand.

"Are you okay?"

She frowned with her hand on her abdomen. "That hurt."

"You get on top so you're in control," Brock told her.

That seemed to work. There wasn't any more pain. She rode him exactly the way she wanted to while he watched. She knew that he loved the feel of her hair brushing against his thighs when she was on top of him, so she tilted her head back and let her long hair slip across the tops of his legs.

Harder, faster, deeper, stronger—he let her choose the pace and the rhythm. So close, so close… Casey opened her eyes to find Brock staring at her.

"Come with me." Casey put her hands on his chest and bore down on him.

Brock grabbed her hips and pushed her down onto his erection—faster and faster, harder and harder.

Casey dug her fingernails into his chest and tossed her head back at the same time he thrust all the way up inside her. Together, they climaxed, and Casey heard herself scream so loudly that it was fortunate that they didn't have close neighbors to hear her.

She collapsed on top of her lover, completely satisfied and happy.

"God I love you, Casey." Brock held her closely, his fingers in her wet hair.

She loved how this man felt, how he smelled, the sound of his voice, the way he loved her with his words and with his body.

"I love you."

Simple. To the point. True.

Later that night, after they had made love again, Brock was propped up on pillows and holding her in his arms. He was rubbing her back with his strong hands, kneading her shoulder muscles and making her moan in an entirely different way.

"Do you want babies, Casey?"

"Yes," she murmured, not wanting him to stop the massage.

"Soon?"

"Yes." She turned her head so it was flat on his fuzzy chest.

"I'll give you as many babies as you want," Brock promised her. "Motherhood is going to look so good on you."

"Fatherhood already looks good on you."

They talked about the future and how the logistics could work. Casey had her condo in Chicago that needed to be leased or sold and then there was her job she had to consider. She loved her school. She loved her fellow educators. She loved her students. It would be hard to give up everything she had built there and start anew in Helena. But at least she had the type of career that could be translated to even a small community like Helena, Montana. She had to work. Even after they started a family—work would always be an important part of her life. Casey broached the topic of Clint and the tension it was causing with her sister, and to Brock's credit, he promised that he would try, for her sake, to forge a different path, a better path, with his stepbrother.

And, most important on his end of things, there was Hannah. She needed time to adjust to the reality of the divorce. Yes, her mother had been living in California for a while, but the divorce had officially ended that chapter. It wouldn't be right for her—for any of them—for Brock to jump right back into a marriage with Casey. And Casey had always believed that Brock needed time to process the end of his first marriage. Of course, she was concerned about her fertility window. Yes, she was still young enough to bear a child, but the clock was ticking. But, at least for now, she just wanted to enjoy the time she had left of her summer vacation, having fun and making love with Brock.

Casey had been in a deep sleep, curled onto her side with Brock's warm body pressed against her. A sharp, stabbing pain, like an ice pick being shoved into her stomach, made her jerk away from Brock. She lurched forward, eyes open, hands pressed into her abdomen.

"Oh!" she cried out. Her loud cry awakened Brock.

"What's wrong?" He knocked items off the bedside table on his way to switching on the light.

Casey pushed herself to the edge of the bed. "I don't know! I don't *know*!"

She got herself out of bed and ran to the bathroom. She slammed the door shut behind her and locked it.

Brock had followed her and was outside the door

calling her name. "Casey." He knocked on the door. "Casey!"

Casey crumpled onto the floor holding her stomach— the pain was so strong that she felt like she was going to pass out or be sick.

"I'll be out in a minute!" she tried to reassure Brock.

Through her tears, Casey noticed a large spot of blood on the nightshirt she had put on right before she'd gone to sleep.

"Casey! Did you get your period? There's blood on the sheets."

"I don't think so…" She forced herself to stand up so she could get herself cleaned up. "It's not time."

Putting off going to the gynecologist was no longer an option. Taylor talked the receptionist into squeezing Casey in for an appointment the day after she had started the irregular bleeding. She had experienced spotting and pain before, but had always chalked it up to her diagnosis of endometriosis and nothing more. Even the times when the sex with Brock was a little painful, she had always attributed it to her previous diagnosis. But this pain and this bleeding were *not normal*.

The doctor took her history, conducted a pelvic exam, made contact with her recently fired, but not yet replaced, gynecologist and collected urine and blood. Brock and Taylor didn't hesitate to put aside their differences and focus on Casey. Brock waited in the waiting room while Taylor held her sister's hand through the transvaginal ultrasound and an endometrial biopsy.

Several days later, the tests results were back and she was back in Dr. Hall's office with Taylor by her side and Brock in the waiting room. But even after the doctor gave her a diagnosis, explained her treatment options and then gave her some time to process the information with her sister, Casey's mind had gone completely blank. There was a noise in her head like a TV station that had just gone off the air—and she could hear her sister talking to her, but it sounded like she was talking to her with a tin can on a string.

"I have to go talk to Brock," Casey finally said after a minute of staring at a jar of tongue depressors on the table across the room.

"Okay." Taylor stood up and put her arm around Casey's shoulders. "Let's go talk to Brock."

Brock wasn't sitting down where they had left him. He was standing just outside the door, pacing on the sidewalk in front of the doctor's office. Casey finished her business with the receptionist before she went outside to see Brock.

"Hey!" Brock spotted her and came immediately to her side. "What did the doctor say?"

"Um…" Casey slipped her hand into his. "I'd rather tell you after we get in the truck, okay?"

Casey saw Brock and Taylor exchange a look. Taylor hugged her sister and said, "I'm going to let the two of you be alone. Call me the minute you get back to the ranch, Casey. We have to figure out our next steps."

Casey hugged her sister tightly, so grateful for her. "I will."

It was nice to see Taylor and Brock rally during a crisis—it made her feel like there was hope for them to all be able to get along. Taylor surprised both of them by hugging Brock before she got into her truck and drove away.

Once they were inside the truck, Brock turned toward her and stared at her face intently.

"Tell me—what's going on?"

Casey held his hand—glad for the comfort she received from the warm strength of his fingers and hoping to give him some comfort in return.

"I have cancer," she told him simply. "Endometrial cancer."

Chapter Fifteen

Brock didn't waver in his resolve to accompany her back to Chicago. They were both so stunned by her diagnosis that most of the movement was muscle memory—making plane reservations, making arrangements for the animals to be cared for on the farm and making sure she was packed and ready to go back to Chicago. Brock picked up the tab for the rush-order tickets to get them from the Helena airport into O'Hare. Casey insisted that she pay him back for the expense of the tickets, but Brock refused to argue with her about it.

"Let's just get you home," he had told her. "The rest can wait."

The day that she was scheduled to leave Montana, Casey sat down one last time in the window seat. This had been a favorite spot—a little cubby tucked away that had an amazing view of the world below. She had watched Brock work from that window—and she had began to admire the man from this window seat.

"I'm going to miss this place," Casey said to the poodle that had been glued to her side. He sensed something was wrong.

"Are you ready?" Brock walked through the door to the loft.

Casey nodded as she stood up. "All I have is the trunk and this one bag."

Brock made short work of loading her trunk and bag into his truck. They dropped Ladybug off with Kay Lynn—she was familiar and would love the Labrador like her own while Brock was gone. Taylor had wanted to accompany her back to Chicago, but she finally conceded that Brock had more freedom to travel at the moment. Taylor did, however, meet them at the airport to say goodbye.

"Call me as soon as you land. I hate that I'm not going with you." Taylor hugged her for a fourth time.

Clint was standing away from them holding Penelope. His collarbone was healed and he was contemplating his next move career-wise. This was the first time Casey had seen Brock and his stepbrother together in one place for more than a couple of minutes.

"Let me see my beautiful niece for a minute." Casey took Penny in her arms and hugged her and kissed her sweet-smelling skin.

"Thank you for taking such good care of my sister, Clint," she said to her brother-in-law before she gave Penny one last kiss on the top of the head and handed her back to her father.

"You get yourself squared away right quick." Clint pulled her in for a hug.

"That's the plan," she reassured him.

Taylor had tears in her eyes, even though Casey had explicitly told her sister *no tears*. Taylor wiped the tears off her cheeks and looked as if she was trying to rein in her emotions.

"Nick is picking you up from O'Hare?" her sister asked.

"That's what Mom said."

Their brother, Nick, had just graduated from law school and was studying for the bar exam. He still lived in Chicago and would meet them at the airport and take them straight to their parents' house in Lincoln Park. Her father and mother insisted that she stay with them until her health improved and she was grateful. The idea of being alone in her tiny one-bedroom apartment while she treated the cancer didn't appeal to her at all.

She knew she had cancer. She believed the diagnosis, even though she would be paying close attention to the second opinion when she visited the gynecological oncologist. But she suspected that she was in shock—she hadn't cried. Not once. She had systematically figured out the next steps she needed to take and then put her plan in motion. Perhaps her brain was giving her a break—perhaps her brain knew that home was the better place to have an emotional crisis.

"Thank you, Brock." Taylor, for the second time in one week, hugged the ranch foreman.

And, miracle of miracles, Brock and Clint acknowledged each other, were civil and shook hands before the two couples went their separate ways. Casey managed to sleep on the plane ride back to Chicago—she had Brock's hand to hold and Hercules to share a blanket with. She slept until the steward announced their descent into Chicago O'Hare; Casey blinked her eyes to focus them as she put her seat back in the upright position. She secured Hercules in his carrier and then pushed the window cover up so she could see the lights of her home city as they approached.

"Back to reality," Casey said under her breath. "I sure didn't expect to be coming home like this."

Brock tightened his grip on Casey's hand. He couldn't have predicted this if he'd tried, but he was about to land in Chicago with the woman he loved. Casey wanted him to see her home safely and then head back to Montana. But that just wasn't going to happen. He wasn't about to drop her off and take off like nothing was wrong. What kind of man would he be if he did that? No—he planned on staying in Chicago for as long as he could manage. He had savings— he'd always been smart with his money. He could stay until Hannah was scheduled to return to Montana, and then he would have to go. He was hopeful that, by then, Casey's treatment plan and prognosis would be clear.

"Nick!" Casey spotted her brother standing near one of the baggage carousels. "Nicky! Over here!"

Her brother heard his name and looked their way. She waved her arm in the air. Nicholas, the middle child and all-around golden boy, had always been the star of the family and the apple of their mother's eye. Nick was handsome and athletic and had followed their father into law. If he weren't such a likable guy, he would be completely intolerable.

Casey introduced her brother to Brock; the two men shook hands and then they walked closer to the crowded carousel area to grab the trunk and other luggage. Nick had been his normal friendly, but formal, self. On the other hand, she was completely worried about how her parents would react to Brock. They were still reeling from Taylor marrying a professional bull rider who hadn't gone to so much as community college—and now their youngest was involved with a cowboy. For their mother, it would no doubt feel like an epidemic of some sort. Something wrong with them that needed to be cured.

Their bags showed up in one piece. They loaded all of them into Nick's late-model Jaguar XJ, and merged onto I-90 East to Lincoln Park.

"Nice graduation present," Casey said from the backseat.

"I was going to wait until I passed the bar exam— and then I thought, why not use it as incentive to *pass* the bar?" Nick flashed her a smile in the rearview mirror.

"How's Mom doing with all of this?" she asked her brother, and he knew exactly what she meant. Their mom was a pathological drama queen; she was famous for making gigantic mountains out of microscopic molehills. Give her something like her "baby" having cancer to chew on? She could subsist on this kind of tragedy for years.

"She's already seen her shrink, her internist and located a support group for parents of children who have been diagnosed with some form of cancer."

"And Dad?"

Nick met her eyes quickly in the rearview mirror again. It was always a mystery to them how their father had lasted for so many decades with their mother.

"He's glad that you're going to be staying with them until this gets sorted out. How are *you* doing?"

"I'm okay…" She lifted her shoulders up and then dropped them down with a shake of her head. "I mean, I have cancer—so that stinks. But besides that, I'm okay."

Casey's parents' house in Lincoln Park was a display of wealth the likes of which Brock had never experienced before. The house was four stories tall, with floors of polished Italian marble, curtains made from velvet, crystal chandeliers and a double banister staircase that he'd only seen used in some of the fancier hotels he'd stayed at over the years. There were layers of crown molding in every room, marble fireplaces and rooftop terraces with views of downtown Chicago. Brock hadn't often felt out of place in his life, but he sure as heck felt out of place here.

"I'm going to see that you're settled and then I'm going to head to my hotel—I made reservations at one of those extended-stay places." Brock's deep voice echoed up the stairwell leading to the second floor.

"Already planning your escape?" she asked him, only half in jest.

"I'm staying close by…"

As it turned out for Brock, he ended up staying even closer than he had anticipated. Her mother, Vivian Bartlett Brand, had floated down the curved stairwell in a flurry of diamonds and designer clothes and hugged her harder than usual before turning her attention to the tall ranch foreman. To her utter amazement, her mother took to Brock like she took to a new Louis Vuitton bag. Vivian insisted that Brock stay in the guest room, and if there was one thing that Vivian excelled at, it was getting her way with a man.

Her mother had one of the housekeepers on staff get Brock settled in the guest quarters while she accompanied Casey upstairs to the bedrooms on the upper floor.

"Let Leah do her job, darling." Her mother took her hand and led her out to a sitting area that overlooked one of the balconies.

"Come and sit with me." Vivian patted the spot next to her on a chaise.

Her mom wasn't often affectionate, but this was a rare occasion that Vivian put her arm around her shoulder and left it there for more than a quick second.

"Well..." Her mother gave her head a decisive nod. "They caught it early. You're going to be just fine."

Casey believed that. The doctor in Montana had assured her that it was at the early stages and the success rate of treatment was very high. If she was going to get cancer, it seemed that this was the better one to get. It was slower growing and hadn't reached the lymph nodes. Surviving the cancer wasn't her main concern—the recommended treatment was her concern.

"The doctor in Montana said that I might need to have a partial hysterectomy." Casey looked at her mom and, for the first time since the diagnosis, she actually felt tears forming in the backs of her eyes.

"Well, just think. No more menstrual cramps." Vivian patted her leg with an upbeat lilt in her voice. "Besides—motherhood isn't everything it's cracked up to be, Casey. If I had to do it all over, I'm not so certain I'd choose it again."

* * *

"Are you lost?" Casey found Brock in the hallway leading to the cellar.

"I was." He had a bemused expression on his face. "How big is this place?"

"Four thousand square feet." She walked into his open arms.

They stood together silently, hugging each other tightly. Brock felt so warm and solid and safe. She was glad now that he had insisted on coming *and* staying.

"Are you hungry?" Casey linked her arm with his.

She already knew the answer—Brock could always eat. She took him to her father's fully stocked bar and then called up to the kitchen. The cook told her what was on the menu for the evening with options for other meals if the prime rib he had prepared didn't sound appealing.

Brock bellied up to the ornately carved mahogany bar. "It's like a hotel—I swear I've run into at least three people who work here."

"I know." Casey went behind the bar. "I think it's really embarrassing, but as long as it keeps Mom off his back, Dad lets her run the house the way she wants. Can I buy you a drink, cowboy?"

"I wouldn't be mad at a nice, smooth bourbon."

Casey poured them both glasses of one of her father's best bourbons. She leaned toward him, her glass extended.

"Here's to us," Casey toasted.

"To us." Brock touched his glass to hers. "Why don't you come over here with me? You're too far away."

She joined him on his side of the bar; he put down his glass so he could pull her into his arms.

He looked into her eyes. "I love you, Casey. I'm going to be here for you. That's a guarantee."

"I love you."

They kissed and held each other; they were tired from their day of travel and a bit disoriented from the drastic change of setting. Her parents' posh Lincoln Park mansion was a world away from Brock's modest Montana ranch.

"I'm sorry Mom roped you into staying here, Brock."

Brock kept one arm around her but freed up a hand so he could take another taste of the bourbon.

"I'm not worried about it. I'm closer to you—so it's okay. She's a well-preserved woman. I thought she was your sister. I really did."

Casey took a seat next to him. "She has a great plastic surgeon. Well-placed fillers and Botox."

"Uh—do you do that?"

"No." She laughed. "I'm sorry to tell you that I'm going to wrinkle. Not that I wouldn't—don't get me wrong. But I'm scared to death of needles. I really am. I've wanted to get a butterfly tattoo on my ankle since I was fourteen and I've never been able to do it. I've gone twice to get it done and both times—" she made a cutting gesture with her hand "—I chickened out."

Their conversation waned for a moment, then Casey looked at the ranch foreman's face lovingly. "My mom really likes you."

"Is that right?" he asked with a pleased smile.

"Yes." She nodded her head but her brow was wrinkled. "And it doesn't make a bit of sense. I've brought any number of very preppy guys with excellent pedigrees home and she picks them apart like I scraped them right off the bottom of the barrel. But for you? Vivian had nothin' but praise."

Brock winked at her as he finished off his drink.

"I don't get it. But, somehow...all of that—" she pointed to his cowboy hat and boots "—fits in with—" she gestured to her parents' opulent mansion "—all of this. Go figure."

Three weeks after arriving home in Chicago, Casey had been on a whirlwind tour of specialists and surgeons. A specialist confirmed her cancer type and stage; a partial hysterectomy with her ovaries preserved was the recommended course of treatment.

The hard truth—the undeniable truth—she would never be able to carry her own child. She would never know what it was like to feel a life growing inside of her. Brock was always quick to remind her, however, that a child with her dark green eyes and his height wasn't out of the question. Yes, they would have to find a suitable uterus to rent, but at least there was still hope. So, instead of having surgery straightaway, Casey opted to receive fertility treatments for two weeks to harvest her eggs. She despised needles—but she didn't hate them enough to risk losing the chance to have a child of her own one day. Once her eggs were harvested and frozen, Casey went in for surgery. Two days in the hospital and she was back at her parents' house for recuperation. Brock was with her every step of the way; he had made good on his guarantee.

"Hi..." Casey opened her eyes and looked for Brock in the room.

"Hey." Brock was sitting in a chair near the window. He stood up the minute he heard her voice and came to the side of the bed.

He leaned down to kiss her on the cheek. "How do you feel?"

"A little better, I think." Casey winced when she rolled onto her back. Her entire abdomen was still so sore from the surgery. "Are you packed?"

It was time for Brock to go back to Montana. Hannah would be returning home and he had to start thinking about getting her ready to go back to school. It was hard to see him go, but depending on her body, she could be healing for another month. She wanted him to get back to his life.

Brock sat down on the bed next to her, took her hand and kissed it. "I wish I could take you back to Montana with me."

"I know." Casey gave him a tired smile. "But goodness knows I have plenty of people around here to take care of me, and Hannah only has you."

"You know I'm comin' back for you, now, don't you? I'm comin' back to get you, bring you home and marry you."

"Well…I guess you're going to have to get around to asking me," she teased him.

"You just sit over there and look as pretty as you are and let me worry about the details," Brock teased her back. "And, once we're married, we're going to start working on having those babies I promised you."

Casey looked into the face of the man she had grown to love so deeply. There was a promise in his eyes that she knew he intended to keep. Maybe they wouldn't be able to conceive and bring a baby to term with a surrogate—but at least they had a chance.

"Brock…" She threaded her fingers into his fingers. "Thank you for getting me through the worst of this."

He kissed her hand again and then pressed it between his two large palms. "You're probably going to get sick of me saying this…but I love you, Casey. You're my best friend and I'm always going to be here for you. You and Hannah…that's my life, right there… Hannah and you."

Brock returned to Montana and took care of his daughter; he got her back into her routine, which was a challenge, and he got her back into school, which was yet another challenge. But the biggest challenge for the rancher was being without his woman. Yes, they talked on the phone, they saw each other through video chat, but he couldn't kiss her, or touch her, or hold her hand. He couldn't feel her warmth next to him in bed—he couldn't make love to her—there were too many miles between them. Too many miles.

"Brock!" Casey's sister waved her hand so he would see that she was already there.

He slid into the booth and ordered a coffee from the waitress.

"I appreciate you meeting me," Brock said to Taylor.

"I was surprised to hear from you. You said you needed my advice?"

He did need advice. He'd been trying to convince Casey to put in notice at her job and come back to Montana to be with him and Hannah. But no matter what angle he tried, she was resisting. He didn't doubt that she loved him—yet she always found a reason why they should postpone their reunion. For him, the time for them to get back to the business of being a family of three had long since passed. Taylor knew Casey better than anyone, and that included him for now. It wouldn't always be that way.

"You know I love Casey."

Taylor nodded. "I do know that."

"I want her here with me, Taylor. I want us to get married. But, no matter what I say, she's always got a reason why we've got to wait."

"She's concerned about Hannah…"

"I know she is, and God knows I love her for it…but Hannah misses her. And Casey's talking about working her contract and waiting until the summer to come out. Hannah will be in California with her mother then and we could be right back where we started—except now it's a year later."

"But what do you want from me?"

"Tell me how to get through to your sister, Taylor. Because I've run out of ideas and I want her with us. And so does Hannah."

Taylor studied him for a moment and then she said, "The only thing I can tell you is that Casey can really dig her heels in when she thinks she's right. If you want to convince her that you're ready and Hannah's ready, then you need to get your butt on a plane, go to Chicago and do some convincing in person."

Chapter Sixteen

Casey Brand stepped off the elevator into the reception area of the Signature Room. Situated ninety-five stories above ground level on Michigan Avenue in downtown Chicago, the Signature Room restaurant had the best views in Chicago and it was one of Casey's all-time favorite places to dine. No matter how many times she watched the sunset over the downtown skyline of her hometown city, it never lost its appeal.

Tonight was a special night—she had just received a clean bill of health earlier in the week from her gynecological oncologist and her parents were taking her out to eat to celebrate. She hadn't dressed up in a pretty dress in such a long time, so she gave herself permission to break out her Bloomingdale's credit card. Several hours of shopping later, she emerged with a fabulous cocktail dress that made her legs look longer than they were, her waist smaller than it really was and gave the illusion of an hourglass shape. Of course, shoes and a cute evening clutch to match were absolute necessities.

After working up a sweat at Bloomingdale's, Casey met her mom at her mom's favorite spa for a day of beauty. Her mom treated her to a deep-tissue massage, a manicure-pedicure, a facial, hair and makeup. The whole deal. By the end of her shopping excursion and spa day, Casey felt reenergized and ready to slip on her sassy cocktail dress and strappy, fabulous heels, and meet her parents at the Signature Room.

"Reservations under Angus or Vivian Brand," Casey said to the maître d'.

The gentleman located their reservation. "Right this way."

"Thank you."

Casey followed the man to one of the tables with a window view. She had asked that her father make an early evening reservation so she could see the sun set—sitting at a table at the top of the John Hancock Center was like having a window with a view of the whole world.

The gentleman stopped next to a table set for two and pulled out a chair for her.

"I'm sorry—we need a table for three."

"I apologize, ma'am—let me check into that for you. Please have a seat and I'll be right back."

Casey sat down and enjoyed the view while she waited. Out of the corner of her eye, she saw a man walking her way—she turned her head toward him.

"Brock…?"

The man walking toward her was Brock. Her ranch

foreman was dressed to the nines in a tailored black suit and a soft gray shirt with a beautifully matched tie. He was carrying a single red rose in his hand and he looked so tall and handsome and in control as he walked her way.

The look on Casey's face when she first spotted him in a place where she least expected to see him was worth all of the planning and preparation for this surprise dinner. He'd enlisted the help of Casey's family—he wouldn't have been able to pull this off as well, or as smoothly, if they hadn't agreed to be complicit.

Casey stood up and met him halfway—Brock hugged her tightly, not caring about the stares or the curious eyes. He only cared about holding the woman he loved in his arms again. She tilted her head back, her eyes shining with happiness and surprise—she kissed him lightly on the lips and then immediately wiped her plum-colored lipstick off his lips.

"This is for you." He handed her the rose.

"It's beautiful. Thank you."

Perhaps it was a cliché to love red roses, but they were her favorite flower. And Brock must have picked the biggest, reddest, most scented specimen he could find because it was one of the prettiest, most fragrant red roses she had ever received.

Brock held out her chair for her and then joined her at the table.

She immediately reached for his hand; there had been a small part of him that had worried about her reaction. Had she really been stalling their reunion because of Hannah—or was she using his daughter, consciously or unconsciously, as an excuse? But the love and acceptance he saw in her eyes scrubbed away his doubt. Casey loved him. It was there on her pretty, freckled face for anyone to see.

"I can't believe you're here." She leaned toward him.

"I couldn't wait any longer to see you."

She was wearing her long red hair down tonight, just as he had imagined it would be, and the green material of her dress only enhanced the loveliness of her wide green eyes.

"I've missed you." Casey put her other hand on top of their clasped hands. "I must think of you a hundred times a day."

Their waiter stopped by their table with water, took their drink orders and brought them the menus.

Casey didn't open her menu right away. "How's Hannah?"

"She's having a good year. She has a message for you."

Brock handed Casey his phone; she pushed the "play" icon on the video and smiled as Hannah's round face and wild brown curls came to life.

"Hi, Casey…it's Hannah. Hey—when are you coming back? I hope you like what's on the menu!"

Casey handed the phone back to Brock.

"She has the cutest face! I swear it's the truth."

Brock slipped the phone into his pocket. "She misses you."

Casey felt a twinge of sadness—she missed Hannah almost as much as she missed Brock. It wasn't this way before her summer break, but there were as many people in Montana to miss now as there were in Chicago—her aunt and uncle, her sister and niece, her cousins.

"I miss her."

"You don't have to miss her." Brock looked directly into her eyes. "You can see her every day whenever you want."

They had had this discussion so many different times in so many different ways—but the facts, as far as she was concerned, hadn't changed. On her end, she was under contract for one more year with her school and her kids needed her. But whenever she would bring this up to Brock, he would say, *I need you. Hannah needs you.*

On Brock's end, Casey felt strongly that Hannah needed time to adjust to her parents' divorce. She needed time and they needed to give it to her. Brock agreed with her completely, but they also *disagreed completely* about the timeline.

Brock must have seen her furrow her brow. "We have plenty of time to talk later. Right now, the only thing I want to do is enjoy a great meal and enjoy this gorgeous view."

"It is an amazing view, isn't it? You can see for miles."

Brock smiled at her. "I meant you."

Casey felt herself flush with pleasure. Brock always made her feel like the most beautiful woman in the room—he never so much as looked at another woman when they were together. He genuinely only had eyes for her.

"What looks good to you?" Brock looked at his menu.

Casey didn't pick up her menu.

"Aren't you going to look at your menu?" he asked her with an expectant expression on his face.

"Uh-uh." She shook her head. "I already know what I want. I have this menu memorized."

"They may have something new on the menu—something you may want to try."

"Nope. I've been thinking about the Scottish salmon all day. It's in-*credible*."

"Look at the appetizers…you may want something to start."

"Lobster bisque." She nodded. "Every time."

Brock had stopped looking at his menu; he was frowning at her in thought.

"Why are you looking at me like that?"

After a second of thinking, Brock picked up her menu and handed it to her. "Please look at the menu."

"Why do you want me to look at it so badly?" She laughed.

"Don't you remember what Hannah said to you in her message?"

Casey had to think back to the video, but then it hit her—Hannah had said that she hoped she liked what was on the menu.

With understanding dawning in her eyes, Casey gave him a suspicious look before she looked curiously at the menu. In the middle of the menu, a new dish had been added:

Meet Me at the Chapel for the Rest of My Life.
Marry Me, Casey.

Casey stared at those words printed on her favorite menu, blinking her eyes rapidly to stop tears from dropping into her lashes.

She looked up from the menu and Brock was no longer in his chair. He was kneeling beside her, in the now-crowded restaurant, holding an open ring box in the palm of his hand.

Casey's knees started to shake from the adrenaline being pumped all over her body by her rapidly beating heart. She had known that one day this proposal would come, but Brock had been so good at hiding his plans to fly into Chicago and surprise her, that there was no way she could have anticipated that the proposal would happen tonight.

Brock took her hand in his. "Casey Brand. If you'll let me, I want to spend every day of the rest of my life showing you how much I love you. Will you marry me?"

Casey didn't need to think about it—she already knew what she wanted to do. "Yes. I'll marry you, Brock."

Brock must not have heard her, because he asked her, "Was that a yes?"

Casey laughed and brushed some wayward tears from her cheeks. "Yes!"

Brock took the antique-inspired brilliant-cut diamond ring set in filigreed platinum from the box. Everyone within earshot or sight line of the table started to clap and cheer as he slipped the ring onto her left hand.

"I love you." She put her hands on either side of his face and kissed him.

"I love you more."

Brock had reserved a suite at a downtown hotel, so their engagement night was full of incredible views of downtown Chicago—first at the Signature Room and now at a suite at the Hyatt Regency. Brock had lit candles in the room so they could leave the curtains open and enjoy the twinkling of the city lights all around them.

Brock walked up behind her carrying a glass of champagne. "What are you doing?"

She made a pleasurable noise when her fiancé brushed her hair to the side to kiss the back of her neck.

"I'm sending everyone a picture of us at the restaurant after we got engaged."

Brock took her phone and handed her the glass of champagne. "That can wait."

She laughed easily. "Okay—you're right."

They toasted each other and drank the champagne, and then with the red and green and white lights of the city as their landscape, Brock wrapped his arms around her from behind and breathed in the scent of her perfume.

"I've missed this," he murmured into her neck.

She put her hands over his hands and leaned her head back to rest on his shoulder. "So have I."

Brock moved her hair over her shoulder so he could unzip the zipper. As he inched the zipper downward, he kissed her skin as it was exposed.

"Are you ready to try?" he asked.

She knew what he was asking—was she ready to try to make love for the first time after her surgery? The doctor had cleared her for sex and her stitches had dissolved. The changes on the inside of her body scared her, but she did want to try. She missed being connected to Brock in that most intimate of ways.

Brock slipped Casey's cocktail dress off her shoulders and it fell in a whisper of fabric to the plush carpet at her feet. She stepped out of the dress, standing now in her bra, panties and her strappy new shoes.

Casey turned in his arms; his hands felt hot on her bare skin as he kissed her lips and neck and the rounded tops of her breasts.

"You're so beautiful to me, Casey. So beautiful."

Casey ran her finger through his hair as he rested his head for a moment on her chest. When he lifted his head, she smiled a playful smile; she took him by the tie and led him over to the bed.

"You look very sexy in a suit, cowboy." She pushed him gently in the direction of the bed.

"You think so?"

Casey walked behind him and pulled his suit jacket off his shoulders. She ran her hand over his backside and gave it a little smack before she circled back around to his front side.

"Nice." Brock winked at her when she slapped him playfully on the backside. "Foreplay."

Casey gave him a little smile and tugged the tie knot loose. Brock let her have control for a couple of minutes, watching with admiring eyes while she untucked his shirt, unbuckled his belt and started to slowly unbutton his shirt one button at a time.

Brock grabbed her by the wrists and pulled her against his body. As she laughed at his impatience, the ranch foremen reached behind her and popped open her bra. He pushed the flimsy material out of his way so he could take her breast into his mouth.

She held on to his shoulders and rested her forehead on the top of his head. The feel of his warm mouth on her breast made her catch her breath.

Brock had a devilish glint in his eyes when he lifted

his head. He spun her around, cupped her breast with his hand and then slipped his fingers into her panties.

"Hmm," he murmured when his fingers found her. "Someone missed me, too."

Casey dropped her head back and moaned again. Brock knew how to make her body hum in the most sensual ways. She reached behind her and put her hand over the hard bulge in his half-unzipped pants.

Brock made a frustrated noise in the back of his throat. He quickly divested her of her panties—the only things she had on now were jewelry and her high heels.

Her fiancé stripped out of his clothes without fanfare; he'd lost some weight while they were apart. The ranch foreman—tall and burly and 100 percent male—was a thing of beauty as far as she was concerned.

"Do you want to take your shoes off?" Brock asked her.

Casey looked down at her sexy heels. "Actually— no. Why shouldn't I leave them on?"

"It's okay with me." Brock swept her off her feet and into his arms.

Casey laughed at the odd feeling of being carried naked. "Wait! The bed is *that* way!"

Brock ignored her and carried her over to the wide windowsill ledge that ran the length of the long wall of windows that maximized the view.

"What are you *doing*?" she squealed when he started to put her down.

"Something I've wanted to do since I saw this ledge." Brock put her down on it.

"It's cold!" she complained on a laugh.

Brock knelt down in front of her. "Shhh."

Casey looked over her shoulder—yes, they were in silhouette, but it was highly conceivable that someone out there in high-rise land could see her bare back and snow-white butt cheeks!

"Brock!" she tried to protest again, but he refused to listen. Her fiancé gently coaxed her knees apart, exposing her to his admiring eyes.

When he put his mouth on her—when she felt his tongue taste her, all thoughts of further protest drifted away on her moans of pleasure.

Brock wrapped his arms around her body and pulled her toward him. When she was ready, when she was wet and so sensitive and digging her fingernails into his shoulders, Brock took her to the bed.

"I love you, Casey." Brock lay between her open thighs.

She kissed him. "I love you."

As gently as he could, and with as much control as he could muster, Brock eased their bodies together.

"Are you okay?" he asked her. She was so hot and tight and slick; it was difficult for him to take it slow and gentle.

Casey was taken out of the sensuality of the moment into the fear of the unknown. Would her body react the same? Would it hurt? Would she be able to orgasm?

"Still okay?" Brock lifted himself up a little so he could look down into her face.

"It's a little sore." She was honest. "And I'm worried that I won't be able to…have an orgasm like I used to."

Brock stopped moving. "Baby—we're going to work this out together. If you can't have an orgasm the way you used to—then we'll have fun finding a new way."

His words reassured her and Casey started to relax

her mind and relax her body. Her rancher took it steady and slow—he was so patient with her.

"Are you coming?" Brock asked her in a husky voice.

"Yes," Casey said in a breathy voice, relieved that she could still have an orgasm.

"Damn," Brock swore. "I can't hold off any longer, Casey."

"Don't." She kissed his shoulder. "Don't hold back."

Casey held on as her man thrust into her faster and deeper until she felt his entire body tense above her and he cried out her name. After taking a minute to catch his breath, Brock opened his eyes and looked at her. They both started to laugh.

"We've still got it." Brock smiled proudly at her.

"Yes, we do." Casey was pleased, as well. Her maiden voyage with her remodeled female plumbing had been a total success.

After a quick shower, they got back into bed and drank another glass of champagne.

"It was okay for you?" Brock ran his finger over the four small scars on her abdomen from the surgery.

Casey pulled the sheet over her legs and curled her body toward him. "It was a little sore at first, but after we got going, I forgot all about it."

"Good." Brock kissed her left hand and then looked at the new ring on her finger. "We're engaged."

Casey admired her engagement ring—it was a stone that was modest in size but large on quality. It was bright white with lots of fire.

"We're engaged," she repeated.

"Do you like your ring?"

"Oh, Brock…it's such a beautiful ring! I couldn't have picked out a better ring for myself."

"I did have a little help," he admitted.

"Taylor?"

He ran his finger over the stone that had taken a decent chunk of his savings to buy.

"I should call her and thank her."

Brock took her glass from her to put it on the night table. He pulled her close and kissed her on the lips.

"Tomorrow." Brock wrapped his arms around her and held on so tight. "Tonight, my love…tonight is only for us."

* * * * *

Looking for more of the Brand family?

*Don't miss out on Nick Brand's story,
the next book in Joanna Sims's*
THE BRANDS OF MONTANA *miniseries,
THANKFUL FOR YOU
coming in November 2016 from
Harlequin Special Edition.*

Drake Carson is willing to put up with Luce Hale, the supposed "expert" his mother brought to the ranch, as long as she can get the herd of wild horses off his land, but the pretty academic wants to study them instead! Sparks are sure to fly when opposites collide in Mustang Creek...

Read on for a sneak peek from New York Times *bestselling author Linda Lael Miller's second book in* THE CARSONS OF MUSTANG CREEK *trilogy,* ALWAYS A COWBOY, *coming September 2016 from HQN Books.*

CHAPTER ONE

THE WEATHER JUST plain sucked, but that was okay with Drake Carson. In his opinion, rain was better than snow any day of the week, and as for sleet…well, that was wicked, especially in the wide-open spaces, coming at a person in stinging blasts like a barrage of buckshot. Yep, give him a slow, gentle rainfall every time, the kind that generally meant spring was in the works. Anyhow, he could stand to get a little wet. Here in Wyoming, this close to the mountains, the month of May might bring sunshine and pastures blanketed with wildflowers, but it could also mean a rogue snowstorm fit to bury folks and critters alike.

Raising his coat collar around his ears, he nudged his horse into motion with his heels. Starburst obeyed, although he seemed hesitant about it, even edgy, and Drake wondered why. For almost a year now, livestock had gone missing—mostly calves, but the occasional steer or heifer, too. While it didn't happen often, for a rancher, a single lost animal was one too many. The spread was big, and he couldn't keep an eye on the whole place at once, of course.

He sure as hell tried, though.

"Stay with me," he told his dogs, Harold and Violet, a pair of German shepherds from the same litter and some of the best friends he'd ever had.

Then, tightening the reins slightly, in case Starburst took a notion to bolt out of his easy trot, he looked around, narrowing his eyes to see through the downpour. Whatever he'd expected to spot—a grizzly or a wildcat or a band of modern-day rustlers, maybe—he *hadn't* expected a lone female just up ahead, crouched behind a small tree and clearly drenched, despite the dark rain slicker covering her slender form.

She was peering through a pair of binoculars, having taken no apparent notice of Drake, his dogs or his horse. Even with the rain pounding down, they should have been hard to miss, being only fifty yards away.

Whoever this woman might be, she wasn't a neighbor or a local, either. Drake would have recognized her if she'd lived in or around Mustang Creek, and the whole ranch was posted against trespassers, mainly to keep tourists out. A lot of visiting sightseers had seen a few too many G-rated animal movies and thought they could cozy up to a bear, a bison or a wolf for a selfie to post on social media.

Most times, if the damn fools managed to get away alive, they were missing a few body parts or the family pet.

Drake shook off the images and concentrated on the subject at hand—the woman in the rain slicker.

Who was she, and what was she doing on Carson property?

A stranger, yes.

But it dawned on Drake that, whatever else she might be, she *wasn't* the reason his big Appaloosa was suddenly so skittish.

The woman was fixated on the wide meadow, actually a shallow valley, just beyond the copse of cottonwood, and so, Drake realized now, was Starburst.

He stood in his stirrups and squinted, and his heart picked up speed as he caught sight—finally—of the band of wild mustangs grazing there. Once numbering only half a dozen or so, the herd had grown to more than twenty.

Now, alerted by the stallion, their leader and the unqualified bane of Drake's existence, they scattered.

He was vigilant, that devil on four feet, and cocky, too.

He lingered for a few moments, while the mares fled in the opposite direction, tossed his magnificent head and snorted.

Too late, sucker.

Drake cursed under his breath and promptly forgot all about the woman who shouldn't have been there in the first damn place, his mind on the expensive mare—make that *mares*—the stallion had stolen from him. He whistled through his teeth, the piercing whistle that brought tame horses running, ready for hay, a little sweet feed and a warm stall.

He hadn't managed to get this close to the stallion and his growing harem in a long while, and he hated to let the opportunity pass, but he knew that if he gave chase, the dogs would be right there with him, and probably wind up getting their heads kicked in.

The stallion whinnied, taunting him, and sped away, topping the rise on the other side of the meadow and vanishing with the rest.

The dogs whimpered, itching to run after them, but Drake ordered them to stay; then he whipped off his hat, rain be damned, and smacked it hard against his thigh in pure exasperation. This time, he cussed in earnest.

Harold and Violet were fast and they were agile, but he'd raised them from pups and he couldn't risk letting them get hurt.

Hope stirred briefly when Drake's prize chestnut quarter horse, a two-year-old mare destined for greatness, reappeared at the crest of the hill opposite, ears pricked at the familiar whistle, but the stallion came back for her, crowding her, nipping at her neck and flanks, and then she was gone again.

Damn it all to hell.

"Thanks for nothing, mister."

It was the intruder, the trespasser. The woman stormed toward Drake through the rain-bent grass, waving the binoculars like a maestro raising a baton at the symphony. If he hadn't been so annoyed by her mere presence, let alone her nerve—yelling at him like that when *she* was the one in the wrong—he might have been amused.

She was a sight for sure, plowing through the grass, all fuss and fury and wet to the skin.

Mildly curious now that the rush of adrenaline roused by losing another round to that son-of-a-bitching stallion was beginning to subside, Drake waited with what was, for him, uncommon patience. He hoped the approaching tornado, pint-size but definitely category five, wouldn't step on a snake before she completed the charge.

Born and raised on this land, he wouldn't have stomped around like that, not without keeping a close eye out for rattlers.

As she got closer, he made out an oval face, framed by the hood of her coat, and a pair of amber eyes that flashed as she demanded, "Do you have any idea how long it took me to get that close to those horses? Days! And what happens? *You* have to come along and ruin everything!"

Drake resettled his hat, tugging hard at the brim, and waited.

The woman all but stamped her feet. "Days!" she repeated wildly.

Drake felt his mouth twitch. "Excuse me, ma'am, I'm a bit confused. You're here because...?"

"Because of the horses!" The tone and pitch of her voice said he was an idiot for even asking. Apparently he ought to be able to read her mind instead.

He gave himself points for politeness—and for managing a reasonable tone. "I see," he said, although of course he didn't.

"The least you could do is apologize," she informed him, glaring.

Still mounted, Drake adjusted his hat again. The dogs sat on either side of him and Starburst, staring at the woman as if she'd sprung up out of the ground.

When he replied, he sounded downright amiable. In his own opinion, anyway. "Apologize? Now, why would I do that? Given that I *live* here, I mean. This is private property, Ms.—"

She wasn't at all fazed to find out that she was on somebody else's land, uninvited. Nor did she offer her name.

"It took me hours to track those horses down," she ranted on, still acting like the offended party, "in this

weather, no less! I finally get close enough, and you…
you…" She paused, but only to suck in a breath so she
could go right on strafing him with words. "*You* try
hiding behind a tree without moving a muscle, waiting practically forever and with water dripping down
your neck."

He might have pointed out that he was no stranger
to inclement weather, since he rode fence lines in blizzards and rounded up strays under a hot sun—and
those were the *easy* days—but he refrained. "What
were you doing there, behind my tree?"

"*Your* tree? No one owns a tree."

"Maybe not, but people can own the ground it grows
on. And that's the case here, I'm afraid."

She rolled her eyes.

Great, a tree hugger. She probably drove one of
those little hybrid cars, plastered with bumper stick-
ers, and cruised along at thirty miles an hour in the
left lane.

Nobody loved nature more than he did, but hell, the
Carsons had held the deed to this ranch for more than
a century, and it wasn't a public campground with hiking trails, nor was it a state park.

Drake leaned forward in the saddle. "Do the words
no trespassing mean anything to you?" he asked
sternly.

On some level, though, he was enjoying this encounter way more than he should have.

She merely glowered up at him, arms folded, chin
raised.

He sighed. "All right. Let's see if we can clarify
matters. That tree—" he gestured to the one she'd
taken refuge behind earlier, and spoke very slowly so

she'd catch his drift "—is on land my family owns. I'm Drake Carson. And you are?"

The look of surprise on her face was gratifying. "*You're* Drake Carson?"

"I was when I woke up this morning," he said in a deliberate drawl. "I don't imagine that's changed since then." A measured pause. "Now, how about answering my original question? What are you doing here?"

She seemed to wilt, and Drake supposed that was a victory, however small, but he wasn't inclined to celebrate. "I'm studying the horses."

The brim of his hat spilled water down his front as he nodded. "Well, yeah, I kind of figured that. It's really not the point, now, is it? Like I said, this is private property. And if you'd asked permission to be here, I'd know it."

She blushed, but no explanation was forthcoming. "So you're *him*."

"Yes, ma'am. You—"

The next moment, she was blustering again. "Tall man on a tall horse," she remarked, her tone scathing.

A few seconds earlier, he'd been in charge here. Now he felt defensive, which was ridiculous.

He drew a deep breath, released it slowly and spoke with quiet authority. He hoped. "My height and my horse have nothing to do with anything, as far as I can see. My point, once again, is you don't have the right to be here, much less yell at me."

"Yes, I do."

Of all the freaking gall. Drake glowered at the young woman standing next to his horse by then, unafraid, giving as good as she got. "What?"

"I *do* have the right to be here," she insisted. "I asked your mother's permission to come out and study the wild horses, and she said yes. In fact, she was very supportive."

Well, shit.

Would've been nice if his mother had bothered to mention it to him.

For some reason, he couldn't back off, or not completely, anyway. Call it male pride. "Okay," he said evenly. "*Why* do you want to study wild horses? Considering that they're...*wild* and everything."

She seemed thoroughly undaunted. "I'm doing my graduate thesis on how wild horses exist and interact with domesticated animals on working ranches." She added with emphasis, "And how ranchers deal with them. Like you."

So he was part of the equation. Yippee.

"Just so you understand," he said, "you aren't going to study *me*."

"What if I got your mother's permission?" she asked sweetly.

"Very funny." By then, Drake's mood was headed straight downhill. What was he doing out here in the damn rain, bantering with some self-proclaimed intellectual, when all he'd had before leaving the house this morning was a skimpy breakfast and one cup of coffee? The saddle leather creaked as he bent toward her. "Listen, Ms. Whoever-you-are, I don't give a rat's ass about your thesis, or your theories about ranchers and wild horses, either. Do what you have to do, try not to get yourself killed and then move on to whatever's next on your agenda—preferably elsewhere."

Not surprisingly, the woman wasn't intimidated. "Hale," she announced brightly. "My name is Lucinda Hale, but everybody calls me Luce."

He inhaled, a long, deep breath. If he'd ever had that much trouble learning a woman's name before, he didn't recall the occasion. "Ms. Hale, then," he began, tugging at the brim of his hat in a gesture that was more automatic than cordial. "I'll leave you to it. While I'm sure your work is absolutely fascinating, I have plenty of my own to do. In short, while I've enjoyed shadowboxing with you, I'm fresh out of leisure time."

He might've been talking to a wall. "Oh, don't worry," she said cheerfully. "I wouldn't *dream* of interfering. I'll be an observer, that's all. Watching, figuring out how things work, making a few notes. You won't even know I'm around."

Drake sighed inwardly and reined his horse away, although he didn't use his heels. The dogs, still fascinated by the whole scenario, sat tight. "You're right, Ms. Hale. I won't know you're around, because you won't be. Around *me*, that is."

"You really are a very difficult man," she observed almost sadly. "Surely you can see the value of my project. Interactions between wild animals, domesticated ones and human beings?"

LUCE WAS COLD, wet, a little amused and *very* intrigued.

Drake Carson was gawking at her as though she'd just popped in from a neighboring dimension, wearing a tutu and waving a wand. His two beautiful dogs, waiting obediently for some signal from their master, seemed equally curious.

The consternation on his face was absolutely priceless.

And a very handsome face it was, at least what she could see of it in the shadow of his hat brim. If he had the same features as his younger brother Mace, whom she'd met earlier that day, he was one very good-looking man.

She decided to push him a bit further. "You run this ranch, don't you?"

"I do my best."

She liked his voice, which was calm and carried a low drawl. "Then you're the one I want."

Oh, no, she thought, that came out all wrong.

"For my project, I mean."

His strong jawline tightened visibly. "I don't have time to babysit you," he said. "This is a working ranch, not a resort."

"As I've said repeatedly, Mr. Carson, you won't have to do anything of the sort. I can take care of myself, and I'll stay out of your way as much as possible."

He seemed unconvinced. Even irritated.

But he didn't ride away.

Luce had already been warned that he wouldn't take to her project.

Talk about an understatement.

Mentally, she cataloged the things she'd learned about Drake Carson.

He was in charge of the ranch, which spanned thousands of acres and was home to lots of cattle and horses, as well as wildlife. The Carsons had very deep ties to Bliss County, Wyoming, going back several generations. He loved the outdoors, was good with animals, especially horses.

He was, in fact, a true cowboy.

He was also on the quiet side, solitary by nature, slow to anger—but watch out if he did. At thirty-two, Drake had never been married; he was college-educated, and once he'd gotten his degree, he'd come straight back to the ranch, having no desire to live anywhere else. He worked from sunrise to sunset and often longer.

Harry, the housekeeper whose real name was Harriet Armstrong, had dished up some sort of heavenly pie when Luce had arrived at the main ranch house, fairly early in the day. As soon as she understood who Luce was and why she was there, she'd proceeded to spill information about Drake at a steady clip.

Luce had encountered Mace Carson, Drake's younger brother, very briefly, when he'd come in from the family vineyard expressly for a piece of pie. Harry had introduced them and explained Luce's mission—i.e., to gather material for her thesis and interview Drake in depth, and get the rancher's perspective.

Mace had smiled slightly and had shaken his head in response. "I'm glad you're here, Ms. Hale, but I'm afraid my brother isn't going to be a whole lot of use as a research subject. He's into his work and not much else, and he doesn't like to be distracted from it. Makes him testy."

A quick glance in Harry's direction had confirmed the sinking sensation created by Mace's words. The other woman had given a small, reluctant nod of agreement.

Well, Luce thought now, standing face-to-horse with Drake, they'd certainly known what they were talking about.

Drake was *definitely* testy.

He stared grimly into the rainy distance for a long moment, then muttered, "As if that damn stallion wasn't enough to get under my skin—"

"Cheer up," Luce said. She loved a challenge. "I'm here to help."

Drake gave her a long, level look. "Why didn't you say so in the first place?" he drawled, without a hint of humor. He flung out his free hand for emphasis, the reins resting easily in the other one. "My problems are over."

"Didn't you tell me you were leaving?" Luce asked.

He opened his mouth, closed it again, evidently reconsidering whatever he'd been about to say. Finally, with a mildly defensive note in his voice, he went on. "I planned to," he said, "but if I did, you'd be out here alone." He looked around. "Where's your horse? You won't be getting close to those critters again today. The stallion will see to that."

Luce's interest was genuine. "You sound as if you know him pretty well."

"We understand each other, all right," Drake said. "We should. We've been playing this game for a couple of years now."

That tidbit was going in her notes.

She shook her head in belated answer to his question about her means of transportation. "I don't have a horse," she explained. "I parked on a side road and hiked out here."

The day had been breathtakingly beautiful, before the clouds lowered and thickened and dumped rain. She'd hiked in all the western states and in Europe, and this was some gorgeous country. The Grand Tetons were just that. Grand.

"The nearest road is miles from here. You came all this way *on foot*?" Drake frowned at her. "Did my mother know you were crazy when she agreed to let you do your study here?"

"I actually enjoy hiking. A little rain doesn't bother me. I'll dry off back at the ranch."

"Back at the ranch?" he repeated slowly. Warily.

This was where she could tell him that his mother and hers were old friends, but she chose not to do it. She didn't want to take advantage of that relationship— or at least *appear* to be taking advantage of it. "That's a beautiful house you live in, by the way. Not what I expected to find on a place like this—chandeliers and oil paintings and wainscoting and all. Hardly the Ponderosa." She beamed a smile at Drake. "I was planning to camp out, but your mother generously invited me to stay on the ranch. My room has a wonderful view of the mountains. It's going to be glorious, waking up to that every morning."

Drake, she soon discovered, was still a few beats behind. "You're *staying* with us?"

"How else can I observe you in your native habitat?" Luce offered up another smile, her most innocent one. The truth was, she intended to camp some of the time, if only to avoid the long walk from the house. One of the main reasons she'd chosen this specific project was Drake himself, although she certainly wasn't going to tell him that! She'd known, even before Harry filled her in on the more personal aspects of his life, that he was an animal advocate, as well as a prominent rancher, that he had a degree in ecology.

She'd first seen his name in print when she was still an undergrad, just a quote in an article, expressing his belief that running a large cattle operation could be done without endangering wildlife or the environment. Knowing that her mother and Blythe Carson were close had been a deciding factor, too, of course— a way of gaining access.

She allowed herself a few minutes to study the man. He sat on his horse confidently relaxed and comfortable in the saddle, the reins loosely held. The well-trained animal stood there calmly, clipping grass but not moving otherwise during their discussion.

Drake broke into her reverie by saying, "Guess I'd better take you back before something happens to you." He leaned toward her, reaching down. "Climb on."

She looked at the proffered hand and bit her lip, hesitant to explain that she'd ridden only once—an ancient horse at summer camp when she was twelve, and she'd been terrified the whole time.

No, she couldn't tell him that. Her pride wouldn't let her.

Besides, she wouldn't be steering the huge gelding; Drake would. And there was no denying the difficulties the weather presented.

She'd gotten some great footage during the afternoon and made a few notes, which meant the day wasn't a total loss.

"My backpack's heavy," she pointed out, her brief courage faltering. The top of that horse was pretty far off the ground. She could climb mountains, for Pete's sake, but that was different; she'd been standing on her own two feet the whole time.

At last, Drake smiled, and the impact of that smile

was palpable. He was still leaning toward her, still holding out his hand. "Starburst's knees won't buckle under the weight of a backpack," he told her. "Or your weight, either."

The logic was irrefutable.

Drake slipped his booted foot out from the stirrup to make room for hers. "Come on. I'll haul you up behind me."

She handed up the backpack, sighed heavily. "Okay," she said. Then, gamely, she took Drake's hand. His grip was strong, and he swung her up behind him with no apparent effort.

It was easy to imagine this man working with horses and digging postholes for fences.

Settled on the animal's broad back, Luce had no choice but to put her arms around his lean waist and hang on. For dear life.

The rain was coming down harder, and conversation was impossible.

Gradually, Luce relaxed enough to loosen her grip on Drake's middle.

A little, anyway.

Now that she was fairly sure she wasn't facing certain death, Luce allowed herself to enjoy the ride. Intrepid hiker though she was, the thought of trudging back to her car in a driving rain made her wince.

She hadn't missed the irony of the situation, either. She wanted to study wild horses, but she didn't know how to ride a tame one. Drake would be well within his rights to point that out to her, although she sensed, somehow, that he wouldn't.

When they finally reached the ranch house, he was considerate enough not to laugh when she slid clumsily off the horse and almost landed on her rear in a giant puddle. No, he simply tugged at the brim of his hat, suppressing a smile, and rode away without looking back.

Don't miss
ALWAYS A COWBOY
by New York Times *bestselling author*
Linda Lael Miller,
available wherever HQN books and ebooks are sold.

Available September 20, 2016

#2503 MS. BRAVO AND THE BOSS
The Bravos of Justice Creek • by Christine Rimmer

Jed Walsh has finally found the perfect assistant to put up with his extreme writing process in a down-on-her-luck caterer named Elise Bravo. He refuses to give in to their attraction and vows to make her stay on as his assistant, but he never thought she'd be able to lay claim to the heart he didn't even know he had.

#2504 MAVERICK VS. MAVERICK
Montana Mavericks: The Baby Bonanza • by Shirley Jump

Lindsay Dalton is drawn to Walker Jones III from the first time she sees him. The only problem? Their first meeting is in a courthouse—and she's suing him! Walker has met his match in Lindsay, but when they are forced to work together, they might just have more in common than they ever expected.

#2505 ROPING IN THE COWGIRL
Rocking Chair Rodeo • by Judy Duarte

Shannon Cramer is a nurse at the Rocking Chair Rodeo, a retirement home for cowboys. When she and Blake Darnell, a headstrong attorney, butt heads over a May-December romance between his uncle and her aunt, they're surprised to encounter sparks of desire and a romance of their own.

#2506 BUILDING THE PERFECT DADDY
Those Engaging Garretts! • by Brenda Harlen

Lauryn Garrett has no intention of falling for the sexy handyman in charge of her home renovations, but Ryder Wallace knows how to fix all kinds of things—even a single mother's broken heart. As eager as Ryder is to get his hands on Lauryn's house, it is the wounded woman who lives there who can teach him a thing or two about building a family.

#2507 THE MAN SHE SHOULD HAVE MARRIED
The Crandall Lake Chronicles • by Patricia Kay

Olivia Britton may be developing feelings for Matt Britton, her dead husband's brother, but his mother is trying to have her declared an unfit mother to little Thea, the daughter her husband never got to meet. Matt's been in love with Olivia for years and he's not going to let his mother's prejudice get in their way. Can they overcome a bitter mother-in-law and a lawsuit to create the family they've always dreamed of?

#2508 A WEDDING WORTH WAITING FOR
Proposals in Paradise • by Katie Meyer

Samantha Farley is back in Paradise, Florida, once again trying to fit in and make friends, now with the added pressure of her job riding on the outcome. Dylan Turner offers to use his status as town heartthrob to boost her social profile, secretly hoping to convince her they'd be perfect together. Will they be able to handle town gossip and past heartbreaks to find their way to happily-ever-after?

HSECNM0916

SPECIAL EXCERPT FROM

H HARLEQUIN®

SPECIAL EDITION

Walker Jones III and Lindsay Dalton go head-to-head in a lawsuit, but their legal maneuvering could lead to an epic romantic showdown outside the courtroom!

Read on for a sneak preview of
MAVERICK VS. MAVERICK
by Shirley Jump, the next book in the
MONTANA MAVERICKS: THE BABY BONANZA
continuity.

"Dance with me."

Her eyes widened. "Dance…with you?"

"Come on." He swayed his hips and swung their arms. She stayed stiff, reluctant. He could hardly blame her. After all, just a few hours ago, they'd been facing off in court. "It's the weekend. Let's forget about court cases and arguments and just…"

"Have fun?" She arched a brow.

He shot her a grin. "I hear they do that, even in towns as small as Rust Creek Falls."

That made her laugh. Her hips were swaying along with his, though she didn't seem to be aware she was moving to the beat. "Are you saying my town is boring?"

Boring? She had no idea. But he wouldn't tell her that. Instead he gave her his patented killer smile. "I'm saying it's a small town. With some great music on the juke and a dance floor just waiting for you." He lifted her hand and spun her to the right, then back out again to the left.

"Come on, Ms. Dalton, dance with me. Me the man, not me the corporation you're suing."

She hesitated, and he could see his opportunity slipping away. Why did it matter that this woman—of all the women in this room, including the quartet flirting with him—dance with him?

"I shouldn't…" She started to slide her hand out of his.

He stepped closer to her. "Shouldn't have fun? Shouldn't dance with the enemy?"

"I shouldn't do anything with the enemy."

He grinned. "I'm not asking for anything. Just a dance."

Another song came on the juke, and the blonde and her friends started up again, moving from one side of the dance floor to the other. Their movements swept Walker and Lindsay into the middle of the dance floor, leaving her with two choices—dance with him or wade through the other women to escape.

For a second, he thought he'd won and she was going to dance with him. Then the smile on her face died, and she shook her head. "I'm sorry, Mr. Jones, but I don't dance with people who don't take responsibility for their mistakes."

Then she turned on her heel and left the dance floor and, a moment later, the bar.

Don't miss
MAVERICK VS. MAVERICK by Shirley Jump,
available October 2016 wherever
Harlequin® Special Edition books and ebooks are sold.

www.Harlequin.com

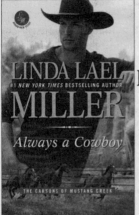

JUST CAN'T GET ENOUGH?

Join our social communities
and talk to us online.

You will have access to the latest
news on upcoming titles and special
promotions, but most importantly,
you can talk to other fans about your
favorite Harlequin reads.

Harlequin.com/Community

 Facebook.com/HarlequinBooks

Twitter.com/HarlequinBooks

Pinterest.com/HarlequinBooks